Mercy's words pricked. "Wait a damn minute. Isn't there something about 'Physician heal thyself'? You're just as much an adrenaline junkie as I am, traipsing around that E.R., getting high on all that power."

She gasped in outrage.

"And what have you got to show for it? An anonymous apartment, dead flowers and not a friend or lover in sight." His mouth twitched. "At least I got a championship belt buckle."

"Cold comfort for a womanizing rascal who never grew up," she said, sneering.

Travis smiled. "I don't get many complaints."

"No, luckily for you, all those young buckle bunnies shoving their phone numbers down those tight jeans of yours don't have a lot with which to compare your performance." Mercy tilted her chin in challenge. "I wonder how you'd stack up against someone your own size."

Dear Reader,

A sexy fire fighter, a crazy cat and a dynamite heroine—that's what you'll find in *Lucy and the Loner*, Elizabeth Bevarly's wonderful MAN OF THE MONTH. It's the next in her installment of THE FAMILY McCORMICK series, and it's also a MAN OF THE MONTH book you'll never forget—warm, humorous and very sexy!

A story from Lass Small is always a delight, and *Chancy's Cowboy* is Lass at her most marvelous. Don't miss out as Chancy decides to take some lessons in love from a handsome hunk of a cowboy!

Eileen Wilks's latest, *The Wrong Wife*, is chock-full with the sizzling tension and compelling reading that you've come to expect from this rising Desire star. And so many of you know and love Barbara McCauley that she needs no introduction, but this month's *The Nanny and the Reluctant Rancher* is sure to both please her current fans…and win her new readers!

Suzannah Davis is another new author that we're excited about, and *Dr. Holt and the Texan* may just be her best book to date! And the month is completed with a delightful romp from Susan Carroll, *Parker and the Gypsy*.

There's something for everyone. So come and relish the romantic variety you've come to expect from Silhouette Desire!

Lucia Macro

Lucia Macro
And the Editors at Silhouette Desire

Please address questions and book requests to:
Silhouette Reader Service
U.S.: 3010 Walden Ave., P.O. Box 1325, Buffalo, NY 14269
Canadian: P.O. Box 609, Fort Erie, Ont. L2A 5X3

SUZANNAH DAVIS
DR. HOLT AND THE TEXAN

SILHOUETTE *Desire*®

Published by Silhouette Books

America's Publisher of Contemporary Romance

SILHOUETTE BOOKS

ISBN 0-373-76067-1

DR. HOLT AND THE TEXAN

Copyright © 1997 by Suzannah Davis

Printed in U.S.A.

Books by Suzannah Davis

Silhouette Desire

A Christmas Cowboy #903
The Rancher and the Redhead #947
Gabriel's Bride #1041
Dr. Holt and the Texan #1067

SUZANNAH DAVIS

Award-winning author Suzannah Davis is a Louisiana native who loves small-town life, daffodils and writing stories full of love and laughter. A firm believer in happy endings, she has three children.

One

"Hello, darlin'."

The sexy rumble of a deep masculine voice brought Dr. Mercedes Lee Holt up short in the emergency room cubicle of Ft. Worth's John Peter Smith Hospital. The man propped on the gurney in front of her had a devilish gleam in his dark eyes and a red-soaked bandage pressed to his temple.

She took in raven hair, an ebony Western shirt with pearl snaps, opened to reveal a swath of spectacular masculine chest, and a championship belt buckle the size of a pancake. Dust-coated cowboy boots, complete with—God help her!—roweled silver spurs, hung off the end of the examination table. Grime and blood obscured the patient's features, except for a wide, come-hither grin beneath his thick black mustache.

Oh, Lord, it was going to be one of those nights!

She mentally kicked herself for failing to take the time

to tuck her honey-colored curls into her usual severe top-knot. Though the grueling pace of an E.R. physician often made her feel she looked twice her thirty-three years, there was inevitably some macho smart aleck who thought it would be amusing to try to make time while the pretty lady doc patched him up.

Make it the day before Halloween, a Saturday night to boot, then top that with a full moon, and what you got was a harried staff trying to deal with a waiting room overflowing with a multitude of wackos and every conceivable type of emergency.

What she *didn't* need right now was a wise guy with an attitude.

"I'm Dr. Holt," she said, her voice crisp. She caught the eye of the brunette nurse who'd accompanied her into the cubicle. In keeping with the season, the nurse sported a green-faced Dracula pin on her pink scrubs. "Lila, what have we got?"

"Scalp lacerations, contusions, possible concussion—"

"Aw, come on now, darlin'," the man drawled. "I know it's been a long time, but how about a kiss for an old friend?"

"Nice try, buddy." Dr. Holt pulled a pen light out of the pocket of her white doctor's coat. "Did you get the license of the eighteen-wheeler that did this to you?"

"Don't blame Sidewinder. That old bull was just doing his job." He shrugged. "Got my eight seconds out of that twister before he popped me a good one, though."

Stepping closer, she waved the light in his irises. Her lip curled. "Stockyards Rodeo, huh?"

A large, tanned hand clamped around her wrist, and his megawatt grin was back. "Lordy, Miss Mercy, you're contrary. Once upon a time there was nothing you loved better than a good rodeo."

She tugged her wrist, her tone frosty. "I'm sure you're mistaken. I—"

Mercy. She blinked. No one had called her that in years. She was Dr. Holt, or Lee to her peers, not that she had time or inclination to be on a first-name basis with more than a handful, anyway. But Mercy was her hometown name, an appellation she'd left behind in Flat Fork, Texas, a long time and several heartaches ago....

Mercy looked into the cowboy's laughing, coffee-colored eyes. The world tilted suddenly, and vertigo sent her spinning back fifteen years in space and time. She recognized him now, even under the coating of dirt and lingering blood. His strong features had matured and changed into something devastatingly handsome, yet still familiar, still dear.

She gasped. "Travis?"

Releasing her, he settled back, his tone satisfied. "'Bout time, blue eyes."

"How...why...?" Spluttering, her heart pounding in her chest, she could only repeat the obvious. "Travis King. Oh, my God."

"Would you like the suture tray now, Doctor?" Lila asked.

Dragging her gaze away from her patient, Mercy shook her head, dazed. "What? Oh, yes, of course. Sorry. Mr. King is an old friend from home. It's been a while, hasn't it, Travis?"

"Too long, darlin'."

There wasn't any of his easy teasing in those husky words, and that startled her. Rattled, she let her gaze slide away from his, afraid of what she might see. Long ago she'd counted on Travis King for just about everything, back when she'd been Flat Fork's pampered darling, and she and Travis's best friend, Kenny Preston, had been in love.

But that was before everything changed.

Before the memories could overwhelm her, she forced them down, making herself brisk again, carefully peeling off the soaked bandage. "Let me see what you've done to yourself, cowboy."

"Just a little knot on the old noggin." He dismissed his injury with a shrug, but he couldn't suppress an involuntary grimace as he favored his side. "Tried to tell those medics over at the arena, but they wouldn't listen. Had a hell of a time convincing them I didn't need a damned ambulance."

"Better safe than sorry."

"I'm not complaining." He grinned. "In fact, I ought to send them a gilt-edged thank-you note. Not only did I get my share of prize money, but now I've ended up in the hands of the most beautiful woman ever to come out of Flat Fork. All in all, I'd say this was my lucky day."

She gave him a suspicious look. "Are you by any chance flirting with me, Travis King?"

The corners of his eyes crinkled with an irresistible little-boy mischief. "Now, darlin'..."

"Can it, Casanova. I can see you haven't changed a lick. And my days as a buckle bunny are long gone." She frowned over the ragged laceration that ran from his temple up into his hairline, now slowly oozing blood. "You took quite a blow. How many fingers am I holding up?"

"Fingers? What fingers?"

Mercy turned to the nurse. "Order X rays for Mr. King. Full head series."

"Hey, I was just kidding!" he protested, dodging and swearing under his breath as the efficient nurse swabbed his face and cleaned the tender scalp wound.

"I don't play around with this kind of injury, Travis," Mercy said severely. "Head ache?"

"Some," he admitted.

"I'll order a painkiller. Slip out of your shirt and let me have a look at that side. Did you get stepped on?"

"It's just bruised," he muttered, defensive.

"Let me be the judge of that."

Travis gave Mercy a baleful look. "My, my, my. Look at Miss Mercy, all grown up and throwing her weight around. Who'd have thought?"

"Hey, you. Don't mess with me," she replied lightly. "I run with the big dogs now."

With a show of reluctance, he slid his arms out of the garment and handed it over. Mercy tossed it into a nearby chair where a well-worn black felt cowboy hat rested crown down, a position dictated, she knew, by cowboy superstition so the luck in the hat wouldn't run out. And bull riders needed all the luck they could get.

Turning back, Mercy caught her breath. While she dealt with human bodies all the time, she was female enough to acknowledge that bare-chested, clad only in black jeans and well-worn Western boots, Travis King was a magnificent male specimen who could turn any woman's head.

Lean and rangy from years of hard physical activity, at thirty-six he still had the broad shoulders, tapering to a washboard stomach, that would be the envy of many a younger man. A light sprinkling of dark hair covered his chest in an inverted triangle, disappearing below the dimple of his navel. In the old days he'd never lacked for female company, and now, even bruised and battered, he radiated masculinity in potent waves. Mercy noted that Lila was certainly an appreciative and receptive audience for all that male magnetism.

But that was a line of thought she shouldn't be pursuing. Instead she drew her attention to the business at hand and pressed Travis's side. "Does this hurt?"

"Uh-uh. Well, not too bad."

"Hmm." Swiftly she continued her examination—arms, legs, ribs—then took her stethoscope and listened to his heart and lungs. His skin felt warm and velvety to the touch, stretched over well-honed muscles with the tensile strength of steel in their fibers. Beneath the pungent odor of antiseptic that permeated the hospital, she could smell the musk of his scent, clean and masculine and subtly arousing.

Appalled, Mercy clamped down on her involuntary response. What was the matter with her? Just because her love life was nonexistent, she was still a professional, for goodness sake, not some first-year student with overactive hormones. And this was Travis—confidant of her youth, part-time Cupid and general good guy. How many times had he helped her meet Kenny when her parents had forbidden it? How many times had she cried on his shoulder when the path of true love ran crooked?

It was the shock of seeing him again after all this time that was making her so jittery, that was all. That and the knowledge that they hadn't spoken since Kenny's funeral. An unexpected resurgence of long-dormant hurt and resentment produced a wince of pain, quickly and fiercely squelched. No, she wouldn't go down that path again. She was over all that, and she had a job to do.

A breathless nurse appeared at the door, hesitated just long enough to give the bare-chested cowboy a wide-eyed once-over, then blurted, "Dr. Holt, there's a possible gastric ulcer in room four and an OB in five. Can you come?"

"Be right there, Sandy. Lila, go help." The two nurses rushed to the next patient.

Feeling the surge of exhilarating pressure that made her both love and hate her work, Mercy swiftly completed the exam, asking questions, checking reflexes. Frowning, she stepped back and scribbled on Travis's chart.

"What's the verdict, Doc?" he asked.

"I want to see X rays before I say for sure. But no cracked ribs, although you're going to have a dandy of a bruise."

"I've had worse."

"I can imagine. We probably need to get a plastic surgeon to stitch your head."

"Oh, hell, no." He waved the suggestion away. "Can't you do it?"

"Well, yes, but—"

"Then go ahead. I got no inclination to hang around this joint all night." His mustache twitched. "I guess I trust you not to mess up my pretty face."

Mercy gave him a sour look. "Thanks for that vote of confidence."

"Hey, for a former Flat Fork High homecoming queen, you've come a long way. It's the least I can do."

His words touched a raw nerve of insecurity that she'd thought had healed. Apparently she'd been mistaken. She lifted her chin. "That's quite a recommendation, coming from you."

"Meaning?"

"Meaning the twice National Bull Riding Champion must be an expert on getting himself stitched up—since it happens so often to the damn fools who ride bulls for a living."

He lifted his brows at both her indictment and the fact that she was aware of his accomplishments on the rodeo circuit.

"Well," he drawled, "we all know the real question is not *when* a bull rider is going to get hurt, but how bad."

Her lips clamped down in a thin line of disapproval. "Not funny, cowboy."

"You weren't always so lily-livered, darlin'."

"Yeah, well, a lot of things have changed, haven't they?" She was surprised at how hard her voice sounded, sharp with an unexpected surge of anger. "But maybe you're right, Travis. Maybe it is your lucky day. *This time.*"

Pulling on gloves, she settled him into position, reached for instruments and a hypo of anesthetic and began repairing the damage.

Stoically he watched her face as she worked. "If that's the way you feel, I'm surprised you still keep up with the circuit."

"Who says I do? Mother keeps me informed about Flat Fork's favorite son."

Holding still under her ministrations, he nevertheless managed to look astonished that Joycelyn Holt, Flat Fork's preeminent society matron and wife of the Honorable Judge Jonathan Holt, might deign to notice a lowly cowboy. "You don't say?"

"Certainly. You're a bona fide celebrity. By all accounts, you lead quite a life."

"Yeah, I've got the world by the tail, all right." Somehow his answer seemed too hearty. "The traveling is murder, though. You know what they say—if the rodeo doesn't kill you, the commute will."

Mercy frowned over the last series of knots. To a healer like her, Travis's jocularity was disturbing. She had proof right before her eyes of the hazards he faced every time he entered a rodeo chute. Not to mention certain other questions that had her professional intuition raising red flags where Travis King was concerned.

"Travis, have you ever had problems with—?"

Sandy, even more breathless than before, burst into the cubicle, cutting off the question. "Dr. Holt, we need you *now*. This mother isn't going to make it to Maternity!"

"Oh, Lord. Finish up for me, will you?" She passed needle and clamp to the nurse. Mercy was peeling off her gloves, already halfway to the door, throwing an apology over her shoulder. "Sorry, Travis. Sandy will take good care of you. And don't you go anywhere until I see you again. You got that?"

"No, ma'am, I won't." Flat on his back, waiting for the nurse to finish, Travis's voice was grim. "You can bet on it."

Mercy hesitated at the door, already regretting her unaccustomed sharpness, regretting…everything. "For what it's worth, Travis, it *is* good to see you again. I'll be back."

One ulcer, a broken arm, a set of twins and a case of pneumonia later, Mercy snatched up Travis's X rays from the pile on the admitting desk and hurried toward his cubicle.

Weariness sat on her shoulders like a heavy overcoat. Thankfully it was nearing the end of her shift, but she doubted that she'd be allowed to get away on schedule. Not that she was in any rush to get home to an empty apartment. She felt restless, unsettled; and the thought of facing another frozen dinner and then falling into her unmade bed, as was her routine, held no appeal.

She stifled a tired sigh. Well, it was her life. She'd chosen it, worked damned hard to get it, and she wasn't complaining. No, she loved the work, the challenges, the rush of adrenaline that dealing with a multitude of life-

and-death decisions every night entailed. Only the rigors of it left precious little time for anything or anyone else.

She thought briefly about losing Kenny, her first love, and about her disastrous marriage a year later. Despite the society wedding of the season, Rick Hulen hadn't wasted much time before he'd left for greener pastures in the arms of another woman. Just as well she'd concentrated on her profession since then. Relationships obviously weren't her thing.

Mercy shook her head. She wasn't usually so morose. It had to be seeing Travis again that had brought on this melancholy. But before she could go home and put this mood behind her, she had to deal with this visitor from her past. It wasn't as though they had anything in common any longer. For all his success, Travis was still a Texas tumbleweed, risking his life blowing around the rodeo circuit. Considering everything, the sooner the devilish wind that had blown him into her E.R. tonight blew him back out again, the better.

Drawing the X rays from their manila folder, she bumped open the cubicle door with her hip. Travis had pulled on his shirt again and was sprawled in a chair, brawny arms across his chest, long legs outstretched in loose-limbed elegance, black hat tipped over his face.

Mercy couldn't repress a smile. During their early rodeo days, she'd contended that he and Kenny could nap anywhere, even on a bale of barbed wire. Both sons of ranchers, it was a part of the rodeo life they loved, weekend to weekend, hitting every competition they could, earning points toward the big time. They'd put thousands of miles on Kenny's old truck before that fateful night.... Her smile faded.

Travis stirred, tilting his hat back to reveal the neat white bandage gracing his temple, watching her as she shoved the films into the viewer. "Back so soon, blue eyes?"

"Sorry about the delay." Chewing her lip, she studied the X rays. "This looks okay."

"Great." Stretching, he stood. "I'll be glad to get out of here."

"Not so fast. I'm going to admit you overnight for observation."

He scowled darkly. "The hell you will! I feel fine."

"From what I can see, you aren't fine."

"Hey, my head's harder than it looks—"

"It's not your head I'm worried about. It's the area of numbness in your leg and back that concerns me." She rattled off a technical explanation about nerve injury and spinal compression. "I'll schedule some tests first thing in the morning and then—"

"Forget it, Mercy."

She exhaled slowly, fighting exasperation. "Who's the doctor here? Be reasonable."

Travis hooked a thumb in his belt loop and gave her a wry look. "The only thing's the matter with me is I've got a hole in my belly that only a twenty-ounce sirloin can plug. When do you check out of this place? We can get you one, too."

"I rarely eat red meat anymore."

"Maybe you should. You could use a little padding on those bones." His grin under his mustache was persuasive, tempting. "I know this terrific little place out on Rosemont. Great steaks, mushrooms in wine sauce, the works."

"Travis, this is important. These tests—"

"Can wait, can't they?"

She hesitated. "That wouldn't be wise."

"I mean, I'm not liable to keel over on the sidewalk, am I?"

"No, but—"

He nodded. "There you have it."

Feeling frustrated, she tried again. "I can't emphasize enough the need to follow up on this as soon as possible. I don't want to alarm you, but the ramifications could be serious."

"Darlin', I'm *not* spending the night in this hospital, for one very good reason."

"And that is?"

With a conspiratorial glance from side to side, he leaned close, whispering in her ear. "Those little gowns they give you. Too drafty."

She shivered at the warmth of his breath and the faintest touch of velvety mustache brushing her earlobe, then stepped back to glare at him. "This isn't a joking matter."

He inspected the fatigue in the set of her shoulders and his smile died. "Maybe not. Look, I'll make you a deal. You let me buy you some dinner tonight, and we'll discuss it further."

A distant tremor of consternation tickled Mercy's spine. Travis was a part of her past she'd put behind her a long time ago. It wouldn't pay to resurrect it. "I don't need dinner," she said firmly. "And you do need the tests."

"Even doctors have to eat."

"I'm not good company after a busy shift. Besides, it may be another hour or two before I can finish up."

"I got no place to be."

"But—"

"Come on, Mercy. Quit giving me a hard time. Unless there's a boyfriend waiting in the wings?"

"No."

He gave her a hooded look. "I heard you were married."

"Old news." Her words were flat. "It was over a long time ago."

His voice dropped, became husky and persuading. "Then for old time's sake."

"I'm not sure that's a good idea," she said honestly, and was surprised at the swift flicker of something almost like pain behind his dark eyes.

"You're a hard-hearted woman, Mercy Holt," he said, joking again, whatever she'd witnessed disappearing so quickly she thought she'd imagined it. "All right, you drive a mean bargain. Have pity on a lonesome cowboy tonight, and help me feed the inner man, and I'll see to those tests in a day or two."

Her teeth clicked together in annoyance. "That's blackmail."

Unrepentant, his expression bland, he said, "It's up to you."

She gave him a suspicious look. "You won't weasel out on me?"

He crossed his heart. "Scout's honor."

What harm could it do? She was a grown woman, capable of spending time with an old friend without letting the past jumble up her emotional landscape. She didn't have to make a federal case out of a simple dinner, even if her nerves were shot and she was as skittish as a newborn filly. At least she'd have the satisfaction of knowing her bullheaded patient was going to receive the care he needed.

"All right, then," she said slowly.

"Gee, such enthusiasm could really go to a guy's head." His tone was dry.

"Never satisfied, are you, cowboy?"

His dark eyes gleamed. "Not often, darlin'. That's what makes me a winner."

No doubt about it. He was losing his touch.

Travis parked his custom, ebony pickup truck with the World Champion logo on the door and the PRCA—Professional Rodeo Cowboys Association—bumper sticker on the tailgate in front of Mercy's town house. The building complex sat in an unpretentious neighborhood not far from the Ft. Worth Botanical Gardens. At three o'clock on a cold Halloween morning, there wasn't much activity anywhere. In fact, nothing stirred, including the blond head resting on his shoulder.

He stifled a rueful grin. Lord, he would take a hell of a ribbing if his rodeo buddies could see him now! "Love'em and Leave'em" King—who could squire his choice of luscious rodeo groupies, who had them lined up by the eager dozens to take their chances with the champion bull rider and ladies' man—had bored his companion into a sound sleep. And after all the trouble he'd taken to change his shirt and clean up in the hospital rest room, too!

Of course, Mercy hadn't drifted off until after he'd plied her with a steak dinner, a little red wine and a lot of cowboy blarney. Sipping his own iced tea—the hardest thing he drank these days—he'd been pleased to watch her across the candlelit table and see the tension in her lovely features melt away.

But what had she thought? That after taking unmerciful advantage of her concern for him, he would insist on plunging into some sort of postmortem of their aborted friendship? He had a greater instinct for self-preservation than that.

So he'd kept it light, and she'd actually laughed a time

or two, something Travis had the feeling was all too rare
for a gal who worked as hard and saw as much wounded
humanity as she obviously did. Still, he didn't know
whether to be insulted or flattered that she'd dozed off on
the way home.

Shifting his weight, he settled Mercy more comfortably
under his arm. A wavy cloud of honey-colored hair drifted
against his cheek. Her fresh floral scent enveloped him,
evoking a deep quiver of something basic and male.
Maybe this wasn't such a bad deal after all. In the plain
slacks and cotton shirt she'd worn under her physician's
coat, she looked slight and feminine, not at all the force-
ful, take-charge doctor who'd bowled him over earlier in
the evening. Quite a transformation.

The reflected glow of the streetlights illuminated the
interior of the truck. Carefully Travis used a callused fingertip to pull the lock of hair back from Mercy's face. He
could be forgiven if he took this minor advantage to study
the heart-shaped countenance, the high cheekbones and
delicate nose. She was even more beautiful than he remembered. Yes, sir, he'd been thrown caboose over teakettle plenty of times in his career, but never as badly as
the spill he'd taken at his first sight of Mercy Holt in
fifteen years.

And he ached. Not just from the pounding Sidewinder
had given him, either. No, it was regret. God help him,
he'd give anything if things could have turned out differently.

She gave a little murmured sigh, and he immediately
felt lower than a snake's belly. She'd worked a full shift,
plus some, and despite his shearling jacket and her wool
cape, the Texas night was getting colder by the minute.
As much as he was enjoying the sensation of holding a

beautiful woman, he couldn't take advantage of the situation any longer.

"Mercy? Honey, wake up. We're home."

Her lashes fluttered, revealing eyes as indigo as a field of Texas bluebonnets. Languid, sleep flushed, she smiled up at him in the dim light, then ran a fingertip over his mustache.

"I can't get used to this."

Her fleeting touch electrified him, and he caught her hand to stop the unexpected pleasure/pain. His voice was rough. "Kinda my trademark now, blue eyes. I'd feel naked without it."

Something akin to horror widened her eyes, and she jerked upright, blushing in embarrassment. "Oh. What time is it?"

"Late."

She placed a hand against her burning cheek. "I can't believe I fell asleep. I'm so sorry."

"No problem." He was already out of the truck, walking around to open her door. "Must be past your bedtime. Come on, I'll walk you in."

"That's not necessary." She dug in her bag for her key. "I'm perfectly all right. But thank you for the meal and everything—"

He arched an eyebrow at her, cutting her off. "No use arguing. You know my mama raised me the old-fashioned way."

He could see her hesitation, but he took her elbow and lifted the key from her fingers. Within minutes he was standing inside the doorway of her town house as she turned on lamps. Somehow it wasn't what he'd expected.

The apartment was spacious, but austere. Pale vertical blinds graced the windows, and even paler modular furniture sat on an oatmeal carpet. Stacks of unopened mail and unread magazines littered the tabletops. A laundry basket of scrubs and lab coats perched on an ottoman. A stethoscope dangled over a lamp shade.

The breakfast bar that separated the living area from the kitchen sported a litter of used bowls and teacups and a cellophane-wrapped bunch of supermarket flowers that had never been placed in water and now lay limp and brown and forlorn on the alabaster counter. There were books everywhere, but no personal pictures. Only a wall display of award plaques for distinguished service for several inner city clinics and a home for troubled youth indicated that the person who lived here had an outside life at all.

"Don't look. The place is a mess," she said, shoving the laundry basket behind the sofa. "I don't have much time for housekeeping or anything else but work."

"Don't apologize. Considering I spend a lot of my time perusing the inside of motel rooms, it looks okay to me. And I know what you mean. I'm on the road so much, there's no time to smell the roses, much less for someone special."

"Don't tell me you lack for company." Her voice was skeptical. "I've had a sample of that potent cowboy charm of yours tonight, and I won't believe you."

He smiled, pleased at her admission. "Glad you enjoyed yourself, darlin'."

She tugged off her cape, looking willow slender and pale and suddenly uncertain. "Ah, I'd offer you coffee, but it's so late...."

He twirled his hat between his hands. "I should be going."

"It's been wonderful seeing you again. Where are you heading from here?"

"Oklahoma City next week. Got to see a man about a bull."

She grimaced. "Travis—"

"No, really," he protested with a deep laugh. "Sam Preston and I are running rodeo stock together now. King & Preston Stock Company."

"Sam? Kenny's brother?"

Her astonishment was plain, and he didn't blame her. He and Sam were unlikely partners.

"Heck of a thing, huh? We're working hard at it. I'm the front man, and Sam runs the operation in Flat Fork. Could pan out pretty well, I guess. You know Sam married Roni Daniels a few months back?"

"No, I hadn't heard. That's nice."

There was a moment of awkward silence, then Travis went to her, his hand extended. "I'll say good night."

She moistened her lips, then slipped her slender hand into his outsize paw. She made a vague gesture at his bandage with her free hand. "You'll need those stitches out in a few days."

"I know the drill."

"And about those tests. If you'll call me, I'll be glad to set them up."

"Uh, Mercy?" Eyes locked on their joined hands, he cleared his throat. "I have a confession."

"You do?"

"I don't need those tests."

She jerked, but he didn't release her hand. "Travis, you promised."

"I've already had them."

"What?"

"Every one in the book, and a few they made up just for me," he admitted.

This time she did manage to free her hand, and her voice was cold. "And the results of these tests?"

He shrugged. "I've got a bit of problem. Chronic, you know, but nothing I'm not handling."

"They told you not to ride again," she stated flatly.

"They told me the risks, but, hell, it's nothing worse than a thousand other bull riders have to deal with, and I'm a whole lot better than some."

"So you ride and risk—what? Permanent pain? Complete disability? Or worse?" Her words were clipped, coldly furious. "Why the *hell* would you do something so completely asinine?"

"It's what a world champion does, darlin'." He lifted a placating hand. "Give me a little credit. I know what I'm doing. Besides, it's all part of the game."

"Game?" She spit the word. "Was that what this was all about tonight? You lied so I'd agree to come out with you. You used my feelings so you could manipulate me. Well, thank you very much, *old friend.*"

"It wasn't like that!" Exasperated, he shoved on his hat. "I just wanted to buy you a meal."

"What it boils down to is that you and your monumental ego haven't changed a bit, Travis King. You aren't a kid anymore. Don't you realize you could end up crippled, or even dead? Or are you so addicted to the thrill of being *champion* you don't care?"

Her caustic words pricked a tender spot, and his temper flared. "Wait a damn minute. Isn't there something about 'Physician, heal thyself'?" You're just as much an adrenaline junkie as I am, traipsing around that E.R., getting high on all that power."

She gasped in outrage. "That's not true."

"Isn't it? And what have you got to show for it? An anonymous apartment, dead flowers and not a friend or lover in sight." His mouth twisted. "At least I got a belt buckle."

"Cold comfort for a womanizing rascal who never grew up," she said with a sneer.

Travis felt his cheeks heat. "I don't get many complaints."

"No, luckily for you all those teenage buckle bunnies shoving their phone numbers down those tight jeans of yours don't have a lot with which to compare your performance." Mercy tilted her chin in challenge. "I wonder how you'd stack up against someone your own size."

Eyes narrowed, he growled. "Let's see."

Hooking a hand around her nape, Travis jerked her against his chest, then found her mouth with his. She pushed at him, her hands twisting in the lapels of his jacket. Clamping his arm around her waist, he molded her close from breast to hip and felt her quiver. Her mouth was hot with fury, sweet with her own unique feminine fire, and after a moment he forgot exactly what it was he wanted to prove, forgot everything except that he was a hungry man and she was his only sustenance.

Softening the pressure, he wooed her, seduced her into her own softening, expertly parted her lips with his tongue and swept deeply into the mysteries of her mouth to taste her essence. Now she was clinging to him, her limbs melting, her lips soft and tremulous, and neither of them knew the reason this had begun, only that it ended too soon.

Travis drew back, shaken and breathing hard, looking into Mercy's face. He instantly regretted what he saw, the pale and stricken features, the swollen lips, the rosy abrasion of his late-day stubble against her tender skin. When she made a little stumbling movement, he released her, and his hands felt empty.

Her eyes were the turbulent shadowed blue of a thunderhead. "You...you'd better go."

It was the least he could do. "Mercy, I—"

She turned away, her shoulders hunched defensively. "Just get out."

He let himself out, somehow ending up in his truck without quite knowing how his shaky legs had brought him there. Numb with self-loathing, he stared bleakly out the windshield, then slammed his fist against the steering wheel.

"Dammit! Dammit to hell!"

He'd blown it. He cursed because he was too much of a man to cry, even though that's what he felt like doing. God help him, one touch of her lips and he was calf-sick with love for the little rich gal, Mercy Holt, just like it was yesterday.

Only it had been impossible then, because she'd been his best friend's girl.

And it was still impossible now, even after all this time, because he'd killed Kenny, and she would never get over that.

Two

Well, she'd always wondered. Secretly, she'd wondered. And now she knew.

Mercy pushed at her disheveled hair, took another look at the unappetizing mess of canned vegetable soup congealing in the bowl, then shoved it across the kitchen bar. She needed to eat something before she left for her evening shift at the hospital, but her stomach was in a knot that wouldn't unravel, had been since Travis King's devastating kiss.

And that's what it had been—devastating. Rawly male, possessive, so skillful and evocative he'd drawn the will to resist right out of her, leaving her helpless and quivering. Damn the womanizing scoundrel!

And damn her for enjoying it for even a moment.

With a low moan, Mercy buried her face in her palms. Instead of sleeping the day away, she'd tossed and turned, unable to understand what had happened. How had things gotten out of hand so fast with a man who was supposed to be nothing more than an old friend? She'd been justifiably furious at him, but why had she goaded him into something neither of them was prepared for or wanted?

Liar.

She'd wanted.

A lump of guilt lodged behind her breastbone, and she jumped up, dumping the soup down the disposal. If she were the least bit honest with herself, she had to admit that much. Since she was seventeen, despite the fact she was Kenny Preston's girl, she'd watched Travis using his prodigious charm on the ladies and wondered if all the rumors she'd heard whispered about him in the girls' locker room were true. She'd almost found out once, and it seemed now that the silly, spoiled, rebellious child she'd been back then still lived too near the surface for comfort. A wave of self-disgust washed over her.

Grow up, Mercy.

A clutter of dirty dishes spilled over the sink, and she knew she should load them into the dishwasher, but the task seemed too monumental to tackle. Instead she crossed to the sliding glass door and let herself out onto the tiny patio. She breathed in the chilly fall air in a fruitless effort to calm her racing heart.

Car lights danced on the boulevard beyond the brick walls that muffled the never-ending traffic noises, but the air was clear and sweet with the scent of drying grass blowing in off the plains west of Ft. Worth. Shivering beneath her oversize sweater, Mercy lifted her face to the night sky, and the smell of earth and hay caught at her memories with thoughts of Flat Fork and times gone by and damned ole rodeos. Vividly she remembered that night years ago....

The shabby motel room had echoed with the deafening crash of the door slamming behind her furious beau.

"Why does Kenny act like that?"

Mercy's voice was plaintive, querulous with incipient tears.

"You shouldn't have surprised him, coming here like this," Travis said. Bare-chested in hastily pulled-on jeans, sleep groggy and bruised from the day's bull-riding competition, Travis eyed Mercy with the weary world wisdom of his twenty-one years.

"I drove four hours to see him," she said indignantly. The room was second-rate and musty smelling, home for the night for a couple of up-and-coming cowboys entered in a second-rate rodeo in a little Texas town. Sinking down on the edge of the lumpy, tumbled bed, she let her lip quiver in self-pity. "Sometimes I think he doesn't like me at all."

"He's crazy about you."

"Then why'd he run off?"

Travis sighed and leaned one hip against a plastic-topped dresser littered with empty beer bottles. "Kenny doesn't like this sneaking around."

"I'm not sneaking!"

"It's the damned middle of the night, gal. Your folks know where you are?"

Guilt heated her cheeks, and she smoothed her hands down the front of her skin-tight jeans. "Not exactly."

He lifted a dark eyebrow. "Or that you hauled butt way out here all alone in that fancy convertible of yours?"

She tossed her honey blond hair out of her face and tilted her chin at a belligerent angle. "I'm eighteen years old. I can do what I want."

"It doesn't make it any easier for a proud man like Kenny, having the Honorable Judge Holt think he isn't good enough to court his daughter. And you acting like it, too, with this kind of shenanigan.''

"My parents don't understand," she said, sullen. "It's not my fault they're living in the Stone Age.''

"Grow up, Mercy. Adults don't deal with each other that way. If you were honest with them—''

"Don't treat me like a child, Travis. That's what *my parents* do. They never listen to what I say about any-thing—not med school or my friends or getting out of boring Flat Fork.''

"They just don't want you involved with a rodeo bum, and I can't say that I blame them. Hell knows we ain't got much in the way of job security. And maybe defying them is part of Kenny's appeal for you.''

She gasped, stung. "What a despicable thing to say! I'm in love with him.''

"Yeah, well, sometimes you got a funny way of show-ing it, darlin'. You put him in a bad position. When are you going to learn to think first, act later?''

His condemnation sent a hot and startling prickle of tears surging behind her eyelids. Travis had been their intermediary time and again, the one whom she'd trusted to convey the most precious secrets of her heart, and now to find he'd been a reluctant and disapproving ally was a betrayal almost as potent as Kenny's walking out. Maybe more.

Her words rasped with hurt. "If you disapprove so much, why have you tried to help us make this relation-ship work?''

Travis shrugged. "He's my best friend.''

"And he's the man I love,'' she avowed, with force enough to squelch any doubts. Thwarted, resentful, the tears spilled over. "And now you're telling me he hates me just because I wanted to see him. I can't do anything right. Oh, God, what am I going to do?"

Sobbing, she collapsed onto the crumpled bedspread and curled into a ball of sheer misery.

"Aw, stop, darlin'. Don't cry, blue eyes." The bed sank under Travis's weight, and rope-callused hands lifted her, cradling her against his bare chest. "Mercy, I can't stand it when you cry."

"Why does love have to hurt so much?" Weeping, she clung to him, her tears raining onto his bronzed shoulder. He was hard and muscular and smelled intoxicatingly of soap from his shower and healthy male musk.

His voice rumbled rough as gravel. "Love can't help where it lands sometimes, I reckon."

"But why can't he understand? You do, don't you, Travis?" Hiccoughing on a ragged sob, she looked up at him through tear-blurred eyes. "You're a better friend than he is. Sometimes I wish—"

"Hush, don't cry anymore." He pressed a comforting kiss against her temple, his palm soothing as he stroked her bare arm from shoulder to elbow, his fingertips slipping under the strap of her lace-edged tank top.

Mercy's breath caught, and she shuddered, her skin quivering beneath his touch. Suddenly there wasn't enough air in the room, as if a flash of heat lightning had consumed all the oxygen.

Murmuring soothing nothings, he brushed his mouth over the corner of her eye, sipping the salty essence of her tears, and Mercy's lips parted in a silent exhalation of surprise and anticipation...of what? She didn't know, could only wait suspended, her middle turning to jelly at the feather touch of his carved male lips, her heart thumping against her ribs so hard she knew he could hear it.

He seemed to be waiting, too, his mouth now hovering

mere inches from hers, his coffee-colored eyes hooded and mysterious. Their breaths mingled, warm and uneven across flushed skin, and Travis's fingers tightened on her arm, his knuckles barely brushing the underside of her breast through the thin knit of her top.

Confused, shamefully aroused, Mercy's head spun. She couldn't be feeling this, could she? This utter longing to have his mouth sealed on hers, to experience his taste on her tongue. But this was Travis! Best friend to the man she swore she loved. Was she crazy, or was that light blazing behind his dark eyes a burning curiosity and need that matched her own ungovernable, inappropriate desire?

What would he do if she curled her arm behind his neck and drew him down to her? What would she do if he took up her offer and pressed her down against the bed? Worse, what would she do if he didn't?

The potential for disaster, for rejection, for utter humiliation made her stiffen, and suddenly the heated light disappeared from Travis's features, masked so quickly by his normal teasing expression that she was sure she'd imagined it.

"Lord-a-mercy, Miss Mercy, you sure are a mess when you blubber." Easing his grip, he dropped a brotherly peck on the tip of her nose.

Chagrined, flustered, she pulled away, using the hem of her shirt to wipe her damp face. Had he guessed where her wayward impulses had almost led her? Oh, God, how mortifying!

"I'm sorry," she mumbled, but she wasn't sure if the apology was for weeping all over him or almost placing him in the awkward position of betraying his best friend's trust.

If he hadn't sensed anything, then it was best to ignore that flash of hunger that had nearly made her forget herself. There was a name they called girls like that, and while she might have a reputation for being spoiled and a bit wild, she'd be damned if she'd ever let anyone call her the other.

"It's okay, darlin', you're just upset." He stood and slipped on a pearl-studded cowboy shirt, then jammed his feet into a pair of well-worn boots. "Look, I'll go find Kenny. It'll be all right. You know he can't stay mad at you for long. You got him wrapped right around that pretty little pinky finger."

She swallowed, not much liking the picture his words painted. "Is that how you think it is?"

"Sure thing." He opened the door and slanted her a grin. But somehow it didn't reach his eyes. "I'm sure Kenny's cooled off by now."

"I hope so." Cooling her own humors wasn't such a bad idea, either, not if she expected her relationship with her boyfriend to continue. But she had to know something first. "Uh, Travis? Have you ever fallen in love?"

He froze on the threshold, his shoulders stiff, then he grinned again, all cowboy cockiness and masculine charm.

"Sure, darlin'. About every ten minutes or so. Only problem is, I tend to fall out again faster'n chain lightning."

Suddenly cold wind whipped Mercy's hair about her face and brought her back to the present. "Every ten minutes or so..."

That's what it had been all about, she realized. Some things, some *men* never changed. A consummate ladies' man, Travis had merely been indulging in a typically masculine experiment when he'd kissed her late last night. Perhaps one that was long overdue. And she'd been vulnerable and tired and as a result, incautious.

Shivering, Mercy stepped back into her town house, blaming the temperature but knowing on another level it was still the aftershock of that kiss that raised her goose bumps. There was a lot unresolved in her relationship with Travis King, things about Kenny, about the way he'd died, about how Travis had disappeared from her life so completely afterward, that she'd lost not one man she'd cared about, but two.

But that was water under the bridge, and it wouldn't pay to complicate her already complex, overworked life by admitting she was still susceptible to a certain bull rider's brand of cowboy charisma. It was a good thing she wouldn't be seeing Travis again.

As if on cue, the doorbell rang. She knew who it was before she opened the door, but she wasn't prepared for the sheepish expression on Travis's handsome face or the giant bouquet of hothouse blossoms he thrust at her.

"I came to apologize."

"Uh—" Helplessly she stood in the doorway and accepted the cellophane-wrapped bundle, breathing in the rich scents of roses and narcissus. What could she do with a man who laid it on the line like this, who stood there literally with his black hat in his hand...throw his peace offering in his teeth? "This wasn't necessary," she murmured.

His mouth under the bold black mustache was solemn. "To me it was. Your friendship means—has always meant—too much to me to risk with some stupid foolishness. Tell me I haven't screwed up everything again."

"No, of course not." She shook her head, searching for some excuse. "Seeing you after all this time...we were both in a highly emotional state, that's all. No harm done."

"I'm glad to hear it, darlin'."

She gestured at the armload of flowers. "Thank you, they're beautiful. Uh, would you like to come in?"

"Better not." His smile was engaging, rueful. "Wouldn't want to press my luck, and you've got to get to work, haven't you?"

She was surprisingly disappointed but tried not to show it. "Yes, you're right."

"I'll be going, then." He shoved on his hat. "Do one thing for me?"

She bit her lip. "If I can."

"Those posies cost me an arm and leg." He winked. "Promise me you'll stick them in some water?"

He'd commented on that wilted grocery store nosegay last night, the one she'd finally thrown in the trash just an hour ago. Maybe he was charitable enough to realize she'd been too tired to find a vase. Or maybe he assumed the rich girl couldn't be bothered with so simple a task, not a spoiled gal like her who'd always bought and discarded things on a whim, unlike a poor cowboy who had to count every penny to keep up with his entry fees.

Flushing, she managed a stiff nod. "Don't worry, I'll go put them in water right now."

Disconcerted by the bitter edge in her voice, he hesitated, then he shocked her by dragging his knuckles across her cheek in a brief and all-too-disturbing caress. "I'll see you around, blue eyes."

Mercy didn't close the door until the tattoo of his boots on the brick walk faded completely away. When she released the knob, she was trembling. The cellophane crackled in her hands, reminding her with a start of her promise. Moments later, the blossoms safely stashed in a cut-glass pitcher—a housewarming gift from her mother that had never been out of its box until that moment—Mercy picked up her doctor's jacket, checking automatically for her ID badge, pen and stethoscope.

"See you around," he'd said. No, not a good idea. Not with the history she and Travis had between them. Not when her reaction to his merest touch had all the dangerous volatility of a trainload of nitroglycerin. She had her life to get on with—responsibilities, obligations, things to prove.

Not that he'd meant anything by that catchphrase, Mercy thought, as she let herself out of her apartment. No, it was just as likely that it would be another fifteen years before she ran into Travis King again, and that suited her just fine. Because she certainly didn't need a dark-eyed, sweet-talkin' cowboy, who didn't care squat for his personal health or safety, coming around, calling her "darlin'," messing with her head and making her think about what might have been.

Not if she knew what was good for her.

"Who's the man in black?"

"Johnny Cash?" Two days later Mercy was scribbling on a patient chart, the final one of the evening and her ticket out of the E.R. for the night.

"No, not him." The young nurse juggled the charts she was holding, poked Mercy's shoulder and pointed. "That one."

Mercy looked up and couldn't contain an involuntary spurt of pleasure at the sight of Travis King flashing his wicked grin at her. She deliberately quashed her untoward delight, frowning as he approached.

"Travis. What are you doing here?" Her professional concern kicked in, her eyes narrowing on the white bandage still gracing his temple. "Something wrong? Headache? I—"

"Whoa, there, Doc." Travis held up his hands. "Everything's fine. I'm just a lonely cowboy looking for a little companionship. When can I spring you from this joint?"

Mercy licked her lips. "Uh, I don't think—"

"That's it," the nurse announced, slamming the last chart shut with a sigh of relief. "See you tomorrow night, Dr. Holt."

"Great." Travis hung his thumbs in his belt loops. "Come on, I'll buy you some dinner. Or would you prefer breakfast?"

He was so tempting and irresistible. Instinctively she knew he was pure trouble, and she struggled to be sensible and remember that she'd already decided the better part of discretion was to keep her distance. She shook her head.

"Thanks, but I really can't. There's laundry piled up, and I've got some reading to do—"

Travis tsked between his teeth and took her arm, leading her down the antiseptic-smelling corridor. "Not much of a life for a pretty gal like you."

"We're not all party animals." Her tone was crisp, but there was no way she could untangle herself from his grasp without calling attention, and they were attracting plenty of that from the staff and the patients lined up in the E.R. waiting room as it was.

"You've got to stop and smell the roses, sometimes, blue eyes."

"So I've heard."

"So?" He lifted one dark eyebrow.

She relented slightly. "So your bouquet, which I've babied with doses of aspirin, is opening up beautifully. And yes, I've been smelling those damned flowers."

Actually there was no way she could avoid it, for the

scent of roses filled her to house, and each time she opened the door, she was greeted by the sweet fragrance of springtime and youth and renewed hope.

Travis's smile was slow and satisfied. "See," he said softly, "I'm a good influence."

Mercy rolled her eyes. "Give me a break, Travis. Nobody ever raised as much hell as you."

He placed a hand over his heart, mock wounded, his coffee-colored eyes devilish. "Maybe, but nobody ever has as much fun, either. And you could use a good dose of that, gal."

"I'm all right."

He snorted. "Sure you are. Somebody needs to take care of you, so come on. Dr. King's orders."

Ignoring her protests, he trundled her off in his black truck to the Stockyards, now a tourist mecca of shops and restaurants and clubs she'd rarely visited, then plied her with slabs of baby back ribs from Riscky's Barbeque. Afterward he insisted they go two-stepping at the infamous Billy Bob's Texas, where, not to Mercy's surprise, he was recognized and greeted with obvious affection by every two out of three luscious cowgirls who frequented the tourist honky-tonk.

While his easy teasing and cowboy foolishness kept her laughing, and on the surface they were back on their old friendly footing, Mercy kept her guard up against a resurgence of that odd flare of awareness. Like a swift current beneath a still river, she knew instinctively it was dangerous and better left to braver souls to navigate.

Still, when Travis dropped her off at home a few hours later, again refusing her invitation to come in, Mercy was pleasantly tired, but amazed at how relaxed she felt. Flinging herself into her rumpled bed, she realized that he'd been right. Fun was an area in her life that was in severe deprivation. She'd have to do something more positive about fulfilling that need on a regular basis. Only, the last thought in her hazy brain as she dropped off to sleep was that it wouldn't be quite the same without Travis around....

And he was around a lot over the next few days. In fact, despite her repeated resolutions to the contrary, she couldn't avoid him. He appeared when she least expected, then whisked her off to some new adventure, not even giving her the chance to refuse. He took her for a ride down the interstate to blow the cobwebs out of her tired brain, bought her fast-food breakfasts, took her to a midnight cult movie, massaged her feet! When he drove up to Oklahoma City alone to inspect a new bull for King and Preston Stock Company, he arranged for a pizza delivery to her town house to make certain she would eat.

She certainly wasn't accustomed to such attention. Indeed, she felt faintly guilty at the amount of time he invested in her "prescription" of TLC. But there seemed no way to avoid the runaway freight train that was Travis turning on the charm for an old friend, and after a while she didn't even try to get out of the way. And if she wondered at his motives, well, she knew he was a tumbleweed who'd blow out of her life very soon, the same way he'd blown in again. She was just needy enough to pretend that the occasional tingles reminding her he was all man were nothing but an aberration she'd soon recover from. She decided to count herself lucky that their friendship was still intact and take what she could get.

At this stage in her life it was all she could hope for. And down deep she had a sneaking suspicion it was more than she deserved.

* * *

He was a glutton for punishment, that's all there was to it..

Travis jabbed the doorbell on Mercy's town house and wondered what the hell he was doing. He should have been long gone by now—heck, he would have to fly instead of drive to Colorado Springs this weekend to make the opening round—and instead here he was, traipsing around after Mercy Holt like a flop-eared hound dog puppy, hoping for some scraps—of affection, of notice, hell, of anything!

He'd been sweet as pie after nearly blowing it with her that first night—chaste as a monk, hardly crowding her at all. When what he really wanted was to take her in his arms again, to take her sweet mouth under his and see if she was really as delectable as he remembered. In fact, he wanted it so badly he was on the verge of a major explosion. His strategy of platonic friendliness was a ploy, a ruse to let her become familiar with him before he escalated his battle plan to make Mercy see him as something other than an old pal. But how the hell was he going to do that if she continued to treat him like her older brother! He ought to have his bull-battered head examined.

The door swung open, and Mercy stood in her robe, one hand clutching the lapels to her creamy throat, her golden hair streaming loose about her shoulders. "Oh, Travis, hi."

"Hi, yourself, blue eyes." The state of her dishabille and the wary light in her eyes made him wonder if she were naked under the forest green terry cloth. He hooked his thumbs in his belt loops to keep from reaching for her.

"Uh, this isn't a good time." She gestured over her shoulder. "I was just getting in the shower before I have to leave for work."

"Hey, I know I'm a nuisance, but I was wondering..."

"Yes?"

He tapped the bandage at his temple, inwardly grimacing that he was reduced to concocting any excuse to be with her. "About time these stitches came out. Think you could help me out? I've got a big date with a bull in Colorado Springs tomorrow night and I want to look my best."

"You're going—?" She caught herself, but not before he heard the dismay in her tone. Of maybe that was just wishful thinking on his part.

"Yeah, Colorado over the weekend, then back to Flat Fork after that. Some prime stock's come up missing, and Sam's flat ticked about the situation. So if you don't mind playing doc..."

She hesitated, then nodded. "Sure, come in."

As he stepped over the threshold, he could hear water running. "Look, you go ahead and get that shower while the water's hot, then we can tend to this and I'll be out of your hair in two shakes of a piggin' string."

She smiled. "Okay. Make yourself at home."

While she headed off for the bathroom, Travis moseyed around the living area, noticing that not much had changed since his last visit. It was still a mess. Shrugging, he hung up his hat and went to work.

"Oh, my God, what have you done?"

A short time later Travis looked up from wiping out the kitchen sink to find Mercy gazing at him in absolute horror. She was still in her robe, her skin glowing and dewy from her shower, her freshly shampooed hair hidden under a towel that was wrapped turbanlike around her head. She carried her doctor's bag in her hand.

His lips twitched. "I think it's called housework."

She looked at the spotless cabinets, the gleaming sink, the clean dishes in the drainboard, the neatly stacked papers and cleared surfaces in the living area and stifled a groan. "Now I'm mortified. Travis, really, you shouldn't have."

He wiped his hands and hung the damp dish towel over the spigot. "Relax, darlin'. I've been a bachelor a long time. Believe it or not, since my folks retired and both my sisters married and moved away, I've been at the ranch by myself and I've become a pretty fair kitchen hand. Besides, a little help for some free medical attention is a pretty fair trade in my book."

"You think I'm a slob."

He grinned. "No, I *know* you're a slob. But busy doctors are allowed, I reckon. Why don't you hire somebody?"

"I've been too—"

"—busy. Yeah, I know." Coming around the counter, he gave her a hard look. "Darlin', you need to get a life."

"I like my life just the way it is, thank you very much." Mercy reached into her bag for scissors and a pair of tweezers. "Have a seat, cowboy."

"Uh-oh. You gonna hurt me?" He eased a hip onto a bar stool and hooked his boot heels on the brass rungs.

"I thought bull riders felt no pain." She tilted his chin up with a fingertip, peeled away the bandage, swathed the wound with antiseptic, then deftly removed the stitches.

He sucked in a breath at the brief sting, inhaling her flowery fragrance. It made him dizzy. It made him hard.

"That's a myth we knights of the rodeo arena perpetuate to attract women," he said in a strangled voice.

"So, how's it working?"

"You tell me."

She looked startled, but didn't answer as she turned away to replace her implements in their case.

"You know, we can't keep doing this," he drawled.

"Doing what?"

"Meeting only at night like a pair of vampires. When do you get some time off? I'd like to see you by daylight for a change."

She gave a little strained chuckle. "Why...so you can count my crow's feet? Soft lighting becomes the hagged-out lady physician, didn't you know?"

Catching her elbow, he pulled her around, positioning her between his spread knees. He tugged the towel free of her damp tangles, then let his fingers slide down the slim column of her neck. He smiled at her startled expression and the way her pulse leapt in the hollow at the base of her throat. No matter how cool she wanted to play it, she was not immune to him.

"I know you're even more beautiful now than you were as a dewy-eyed kid," he said softly.

She stiffened. "Don't do this."

"Do what?"

"Play games with me."

"What makes you think I'm playing?" His thumb traced the curve of her collarbone.

"Because that's what 'Love'em-and-leave'em' King does."

"Maybe, maybe not." Bending close, he nuzzled the side of her neck, whisking his mustache over her skin, smiling to himself at the shudder that raced beneath the satiny surface.

She batted his shoulder. "Stop it, Travis. You're trying to change things."

"Exactly. Glad you finally figured it out."

"I thought we had this clear," she said angrily. "I know you. You've got a buckle bunny in every rodeo town from here to California. Maybe you're just bored, maybe I'm some sort of unfinished challenge from your past, but I won't be a notch on some cowboy's bedpost. Especially not yours.''

Hands tightening on her forearms, Travis reared back, his jaw going taut. "I don't recall issuing that kind of invitation, darlin'. But hang on, I'm sure I'll get around to it eventually. If you play your cards right.''

"Leave me alone. I'm not interested.''

"Liar. You know as well as I do that something powerful's going on here.''

"Nothing of importance.'' She gave him a haughty glare, the princess withering the peasant with a glance, and his blood began to boil. "Nothing I'd care to trust.''

Her words pricked him in the half-healed wound of old insecurities, the part of him that felt responsible for Kenny's accident. He must have been crazy to think she could have let that go, even long enough to explore a friendship that was more than it should have been and a chemistry that couldn't be ignored no matter how hard she tried.

But then, he'd never pretended to be a rocket scientist. Hell, he hadn't even finished college! There'd never been much he could offer the rich girl, and there certainly wasn't much now. The lick he'd taken on the noggin a week earlier must have made him loco to think he might ever have a snowball's chance in hell with a high-society gal like her—then or now.

He smiled, but he knew there was no humor in it. "Miss Mercy Holt, heartless and cold, same as always. Why am I not surprised?''

"Just because I'm too smart to fall for your cowboy palaver? Well, don't beat yourself up about it.'' Features tight with fury, she tried to pull away, but he held her fast, and her voice dripped acid. "I'm sure there's plenty of empty-headed twits who'll fawn and sigh over the 'champeen' and give you all you think you've got coming. You certainly don't need me for that.''

His smile turned wolfish. "You're right, I don't. I've got a lot more on my plate than catering to a spoiled little witch who never grew up. 'Course, it might have been interesting while it lasted. Guess we'll never know.''

She gasped in outrage. "You despicable sidewinder! You sorry—''

"Then again," he growled, "I hate to disappoint a lady.''

Jerking her close, he covered her mouth with his, consuming her small squeal of protest with a sweep of his tongue. Hurt, disappointed, enraged, he burned his bridges behind him, kissing her unmercifully, holding her against his chest, his body growing hard at the sweet pressure of her against his thighs.

Boldly he explored her mouth, then slid his hand inside the lapels of her robe to cup and lift the lush flesh of her naked breast. Mercy shuddered and clenched her fingers in the black cotton of his shirt, arching involuntarily to fill his palm, and he gentled, rubbing the distended bud of her nipple in slow circles that inflamed them both.

Everything changed in an instant. Summer lightning flared, distant at first, then the thunder was pounding in their veins, and the storm raged uncontrolled, a week's— a lifetime's—worth of wondering and denial unleashed by temper to its full and uncontrolled limits. Gasping, hungry, insatiable—lips clung, hands explored, hearts exploded.

She lay pressed back against the kitchen bar, her robe slipping off both shoulders, his hands tugging at the sash, when the telephone on the counter jangled, discordant and intrusive as a panther's scream in a nursery school.

"Oh, God, Mercy—!" he breathed against her skin, a prayer, a curse, an apology.

Fingers moments before stroking the hair at his nape now clenched the raw strands, tightening at each strident ring of the phone. "Stop."

Releasing her, he stepped back, raising his hands like an outlaw held at gunpoint, horrified and guilty and caught in the act. She rolled away, tugging the robe over her shoulders, and he saw the glint of tears in her eyes and died right there.

"Mercy—"

"Damn you, Travis." The phone pealed, unrelenting, nearly drowning out her husky curse. "You have no right...I can't feel...breaking me open...oh, damn you!"

No, he knew he had no rights where she was concerned, but somehow he sensed her anger wasn't so much directed at him as at herself. But how could that be?

He reached out to her. "Darlin', there's nothing wrong with these feelings we've got—"

She straightened, ignoring his hand, her eyes going icy as she pulled her self-control about her like a cloak. "That's typical small-town mentality. Thank God I got out when I did, and I'm never going back. I don't need this. I don't want you. So go away, cowboy, and leave me the hell alone!"

Snatching up the ever-pealing phone, she turned her back on him and barked into the receiver. "Dr. Holt."

Pierced through, Travis wondered if he actually staggered at her painful rejection. Lame-brained, chuckle-headed fool. Now he'd really ruined everything. There wasn't much left for a man with a grain of decency to do except tuck tail and vamoose, just as she demanded. He was trying to remember where he'd set his hat, when she gasped and her face drained, washing her cheeks with alabaster.

"What? Mother, slow down, I can't—" Mercy's knuckles shone white as she clenched the phone.

Frowning, Travis stepped forward, eavesdropping without shame. His movement made her glance up, but she stared right through him, dazed and unseeing.

"Daddy's heart? Dr. Hazelton at Flat Fork Hospital. Yes, Mother, I understand. I'm on my way."

Three

"We're almost there. You want to stop by your house first?"

The question jerked Mercy from the dark place in her mind where she'd retreated during the interminable, two-hour, bat-out-of-hell drive to Flat Fork. Chilled despite the blast from the heater of Travis's truck, she huddled under her wool coat and peachy cashmere sweater, surprised to find the outskirts of town rushing past the windows.

Sure enough, the two-story rose brick Georgian mansion where she'd grown up loomed ahead. Even in the dark it was imposing with its sweeping drive and two acres of carefully manicured grounds. One or two windows glowed softly behind the drawn drapes, but the house offered her no welcome. It rarely had.

She darted a quick glance at the grim-faced man at the

wheel, then brushed her loose hair back from her face with a wobbly hand. "No. Go directly to the hospital."

Travis didn't answer, just gunned a bit more speed out of the vehicle, then raced down the wide deserted main street.

Mercy turned her face back to the window, noticing vaguely that little had changed in the Flat Fork business district since her last visit nearly a year earlier. The orange pharmacy sign left over from the fifties still hung over the drugstore, and garish, painted prices blazed on the windows of Patterson's Furniture. The redbrick Methodist Church sat in stuffy splendor on the corner, and farther down, centered in the square, the white limestone bulk of the courthouse, where her father had his chambers, reigned supreme over the town.

Her father. Shivering, she swallowed hard, the frightened daughter in her warring with the knowledgeable physician. Oh, God, Daddy. Please be all right.

She felt a hand on her shoulder, a reassuring squeeze.

"We'll be there in a minute."

"Yes. Thanks." Her voice was brittle, her body so stiff she thought she might shatter at his touch.

Might? A bubble of hysterical laughter licked at the back of her throat. She *had* shattered, surrendered, nearly given herself to Travis King right in her own kitchen. Even now, with the anxiety of her father's illness weighing on her, she felt a shameful quickening in her middle, remembering the feel of Travis's lean body, his expert hands, his tempting, voracious mouth.

What might have happened if that call hadn't interrupted them? She shuddered uncontrollably. He'd awakened hungers she thought dead and buried with her first love and her disastrous marriage, and the fact that it was

Travis—whom she'd loved as a brother—made her guilty and mad as hell.

She wanted to kill him.

It was all changed now, ruined, the friendship they'd shared irrevocably transmuted, and for what? A few moments' pleasure? The possibility of a quick roll in the hay for old time's sake before they both moved on? She wanted to scream with grief, but she was numb. How could he have done this to her, to them both, after what he'd said about valuing their old relationship?

Selfish bastard. And kind-hearted friend.

A man who, with one look at her stricken face after her mother's frantic call, had taken complete charge of the situation in a high-handed, typically male fashion that infuriated her even while it brought secret relief. He scoffed at her intention of driving home by herself, then sent her to pack a few things—something that wouldn't have occurred to her to do in the state she was in—while he made the appropriate phone calls to her superiors.

Yes, it was an emergency, and no, there was nothing they could do. Yes, she'd keep the hospital informed, and no, don't count on Dr. Holt for the next few days.

Well, it was an emergency, and even though Travis hadn't given her a real choice, it was practical for the moment to let him have his way. So she'd accepted their unspoken truce. Enough was enough, however, and despite a sexual expertise that broke down all her barriers in a way that was seriously frightening, it couldn't happen again—ever. That much he had to learn. And she was sure that the moment she made that absolutely clear, he'd roll off to greener pastures like the tumbleweed he was.

Travis drove the truck under the lighted archway at Flat Fork Hospital. A sprawling, blond brick edifice, housing only fifty beds, the facility served the rural community's basic needs, with more serious cases being shipped on via ambulance or medivac helicopter to Ft. Worth's larger hospitals. A sign over a pair of double glass doors said Emergency.

"Here we are."

But Mercy was already scrambling out of the truck, only to find the doors locked. Frustrated, she pounded on the glass.

"One side, darlin'." Travis stepped up beside her and hit a button on the wall. Somewhere deep inside the building a buzzer sounded. "They lock up after visiting hours."

"Good thing you know the drill," she muttered, peering anxiously through the glass at the approaching attendant.

His cheek creased in a wry smile, and he shrugged under his shearling jacket. "Ought to. Been here often enough to get Doc Hazelton's discount rate."

At that insouciant reminder of the dangerous nature of his vocation, Mercy's stomach went weightless with dread. Instantly angry at her own reaction, she tamped down on the feeling. What did she care if he risked life and limb? After all, she'd tried to talk sense into him, to no avail. If he chose to be a damned fool, that was his business, and all the more reason to avoid any kind of entanglement. She certainly had other more important concerns to occupy her time, starting with her father.

A stocky nurse, whose homey face seemed inexplicably familiar, flipped the bolt and held the door open. "There you are. Doc guessed you'd be here soon."

Mercy hesitated. "Uh, yes. I'm Judge Holt's daughter...."

"Yes, of course you are. Mercy, you remember me, don't you? Jeanne Potter?" The nurse led them up the shadowy corridor, her soft-soled shoes noiseless on the highly polished tiles.

Mercy couldn't honestly say she recognized her, but then, while everyone in the county knew the judge and his family, the reverse wasn't necessarily true. She forced a weak smile. "Yes, of course I do, Jeanne. I'm sorry, I'm a little rattled."

"Not surprising. Your dad's in twenty-three." At the high-countered nursing station she pointed around the corner, then nodded at Mercy's companion. "How you doin', Travis?"

"Can't complain. Ross okay?"

"Ailing in his back, but he'll live. Thanks for asking."

Travis steered Mercy toward her father's room, calling back over his shoulder. "Sam really liked the look of that last bunch of calves. Tell Ross to give me a call in the spring and we'll do business."

"Sure thing."

Travis's easy manner and familiarity with Jeanne emphasized Mercy's feeling of awkwardness, even alienation, on her home turf. Never comfortable as the darling of Flat Fork society, sometimes her stiffness had been perceived as a snotty, stuck-up arrogance. She'd worked hard to overcome that in her work, and generally felt her patients found her bedside manner warm and caring, but tonight she'd barely crossed the county line and already the old worthless feelings of uncertainty were whipping up into a frenzy. It was truly disgusting that a professional woman of her age and standing could still be at the mercy of childhood demons and little-town insecurities. Thank God she wasn't stuck in Flat Fork anymore.

"This is it." Travis pointed at the sign indicating room twenty-three.

Mercy paused, drew a deep breath for composure, then

pushed open the door. Travis followed her. Cardiac and
IV monitors beeped quietly next to the supine figure in
the single bed. The petite silver-blond-haired woman
seated in the pseudo-leather chair at the foot looked up at
their entrance, flicked a brief, curious glance at Travis,
then rose to her feet.

"Mercedes." Elegantly coiffed and chicly dressed as
usual, Joycelyn Holt's aristocratic features were tight with
strain as she hugged her only child.

"Mother." Mercy felt her throat constrict.

Joy pulled back, inspecting her. "You've got to do
something with that hair. I'm so glad you're here."

"How is he?"

"I wish the two of you wouldn't talk about me like
I've got one foot in the coffin," a voice complained from
the bed. "I'm not dead yet."

Joycelyn sighed. "Cantankerous."

A good sign. Relief surging through her, Mercy hurried
to her father's side. His gray pallor and shallow breathing
behind a transparent oxygen mask caught her by surprise,
but she forced herself to smile as she took his hand and
surreptitiously felt for his pulse.

"Hello, Daddy. Misbehaving as usual, I see."

"Howdy, yourself, Doctor." Propped against a stack of
pillows, Jonathan Holt managed a wry grin. "Come to
take my temperature?"

"Anything you want. How are you feeling?"

"Like a stuck pig," he grumbled. The cotton white
puffs of his eyebrows twirled skyward as irascibly as ever,
but his shock of silver hair lay uncharacteristically flat
with sweat against his scalp, and his hazel eyes were tired.
"Damn quack Hazelton tried to make a pincushion out of
me. Listen, I'm glad you're on the case. Can you get me
out of here?"

His wife sighed again. "Jonathan, please."

"Depends on what you've done to yourself, Daddy," Mercy replied cautiously. "When I see your chart—"

There was a sharp rap on the door, and Dr. Eugene Hazelton blew inside like a miniature tornado, followed closely by Jeanne Potter carrying an armload of patient charts. Bluff, barrel-chested and balding, but still vigorous at sixty, Hazelton glanced at the cowboy hovering near the door, did a double take, grinned and stuck out a hand.

"Travis King." They shook hands. "How the hell are you, son?"

"Just fine, Doc."

"Well, that's certainly a switch," Dr. Hazelton said, chuckling. "What'cha doing in this neck of the woods?"

Travis shrugged. "Gave Mercy a lift from the big city."

"That was very kind of you, Mr. King," Joycelyn said.

Her mother's formality—a reminder that the Kings had never been the calibre of folks the Holts associated with—made Mercy wince, but Travis merely nodded.

"Glad to help, ma'am. I'll just step outside while, er—" He caught Mercy's eye. "I'll wait for you."

He disappeared into the corridor, and Mercy felt heat rise in her cheeks at the others' speculative glances. She turned to the older doctor, forcing briskness into her manner. "About my father's condition?"

Ten minutes later Mercy followed Dr. Hazelton and Jeanne into the deserted corridor. Doc patted her arm.

"We'll see how he's doing in the morning, okay? In the meantime, try to see that Joy gets some rest."

"Yes. Thank you, Doc." Chewing her lip, she watched him bustle away to another patient, then jumped when Travis materialized out of the shadows of a nearby doorway.

His ubiquitous black attire had made him nearly invisible, but she didn't know if the surge of irritation his appearance produced was from the start he'd given her or her own wayward response to his lean masculinity and a magnetism that was undeniably beguiling. What was wrong with her? This ever-present awareness was becoming damned annoying.

"How bad is he?" Travis asked quietly.

"Could be a lot worse." Unable to keep the relief out of her voice, she gave a brief explanation of cardiac function and enzyme levels and how her father had been lucky—this time. Stabilized, with proper rest and treatment, prognosis was good.

Her lips twisted. "This was a wake-up call that Daddy didn't expect to get. He's going to have to make some changes."

"Hard thing for a man like your father."

"Some worse than others," she said, her look pointed. Two peas from the same pod. Then she curtailed that thought. She had no right to condemn Travis or her father for being the way they were.

Sighing, she pushed at her hair. Joy would probably demand that Mercy pin it back from her face, the way she'd had to when she was a girl. She probably would comply, just to keep the peace. And it was time to cut her losses, make what she could of that elusive commodity with Travis and send him on his way.

"I'm staying here tonight," she informed him. "I may not see you again, so thank you for everything."

Travis's dark eyes gleamed, and his voice went silky. "Think you're going to get rid of me that easily, do you, darlin'?"

His words touched off a trill of alarm along her spine. "I appreciate everything you've done, but I've imposed on your good nature long enough. I don't want to hold you up any more than I already have, so I'll let you say good-night.''

A knot in his jaw throbbed, visible proof that her dismissal rankled, but whatever retort he might have made was cut short as Joy emerged from the hospital room. Grateful for the interruption, Mercy went to her.

"Mother, I really wish you'd reconsider and go home. You won't do Daddy a bit of good if you get tired out, and I'm accustomed to the late shift.''

"I'd be honored to see you home, Mrs. Holt,'' Travis offered.

"Thank you, Mr. King, but I prefer to stay. Besides, I wouldn't sleep a wink at home. Maybe tomorrow.'' Joy squeezed Mercy's hand. "Knowing you're here makes all the difference.''

"Of course. Doc and I agree that Daddy should be able to come home in a day or two, barring anything unforeseen. Another couple of days to see him settled before I go back to Ft. Worth and—''

"Mercedes Lee Holt!'' Joy gasped, her expression horrified. "You can't mean that!''

Uncertain at what transgression she'd perpetrated this time, Mercy hesitated. "Mean what?''

"Your father nearly dies of a heart attack and all you can spare him is a few measly days of your time?'' Tears welled up in Joy's pale blue eyes. "That's the most heartless thing I ever heard.''

Helpless, Mercy stared in utter dismay at her mother's wet cheeks. She never cried. It spoiled one's makeup. "Mother, you're overwrought. I simply meant—''

"I can't do it by myself. You heard what Doc said. Your father will have to follow a strict regimen, and he never does a thing I say. He'll be chomping at the bit to get back to work, and then there's that new Juvenile Task Force thing—oh, he'll kill himself for sure.''

''Now you're exaggerating. It wasn't a full-fledged attack, and Daddy's recovery should be uneventful.''

''That's how little you know your father.'' Joy pulled a dainty, lace-edged handkerchief from her pocket and dabbed her eyes. ''I know you hate Flat Fork, and you probably hate both me and your father, too—''

Mercy gasped. ''Mother, that's not true!''

''—but it's your duty to stay as long as I need you.''

''Well, yes, but my job—I have responsibilities.''

''You work too hard, like your father.''

''That's what I've been trying to tell her, Mrs. Holt,'' Travis interjected. He caught Mercy's furious glare and smiled blandly beneath the dark curl of his mustache.

''Thank you, Mr. King,'' Joy said, ''I'm glad I'm not the only one who's noticed. Mercedes, I won't allow you to use work as an excuse. I'm fully aware that you've built up weeks and weeks of vacation time simply because you can't abide coming home.''

Mercy cringed at the guilty truth in that. ''Mother, my career is very demanding. I certainly don't mean to slight either you or Daddy.''

''Then prove it. Stay through Thanksgiving. Is that too much to ask of my own daughter?''

''Three weeks?'' Stuck in Flat Fork. At the mercy of memories better left undisturbed. Caught in the parental trap again. Mercy swallowed on a tidal wave of dismay at the prospect. ''Mother, I—I don't think that's possible or even necessary. Of course I'll be here as long as you and Daddy need me, but can't we play all of this by ear?''

''I see exactly where your loyalties still lie—always with yourself.'' The bitter disappointment in Joy's face cleaved Mercy's soul.

"Uh, maybe I can arrange something," she muttered, backed into a corner and hating that she sounded like a resentful, mutinous child.

"See that you do," Joy said, her voice curt. Turning on her heel, she stalked back into the room.

Mercy slumped against the wall, rubbing at the sudden throbbing in her temple. "God."

Travis dropped a comforting hand to her shoulder. "Hey, you can't take anything she says right now to heart. She's really worried."

"You think I don't know that about my own mother?" Mercy shook him off, incensed, and ready to take out her frustrations and fear on the nearest target, especially one who'd complicated her world and added to her problems and deserved what he got. "I'm tired of your butting into my business, trying to take charge without so much as a by-your-leave, pushing me into things I don't want. I won't stand for it."

A dull rush of red spread underneath his swarthy complexion, and his drawl was slow and dangerous. "Funny, I didn't hear you complaining earlier."

She nearly choked on her fury. "That was a damned mistake and you know it."

"Could have fooled me. But I'm just a dumb cowpoke, so maybe I was confused by the way you were draped over that counter, moaning in my arms."

Crimson seared her cheeks. "I said it was a mistake, and one I never intend to repeat. So keep your advice and your dinners and your foot rubs, cowboy. Believe it or not, I'm perfectly capable of living my life without some guy's overinflated ego and a yen to sample anything in skirts telling me what to do."

"I'll let that pass because I know you're really worried about the judge, too," Travis said, his voice steely.

His forbearance made her feel puerile and petty, and it demolished what was left of her control. "Listen here, mister, don't do me any more favors! I've had my fill and they turn my stomach."

The corners of his mouth twisted, and his dark eyes narrowed. "That's what I like about you, Mercy. Sweet as honeycomb one minute and mean as a rattler on hot coals the next."

"Save that famous cowboy charm for the buckle bunnies," she hissed. "And since I've already expressed my gratitude for the ride, why don't you just get the hell out of here before I say something I'll truly regret."

"Sure, I'll go, if that's what you want, but you'd best remember one thing."

"What's that?"

With studied insolence he brushed a thumb across her lips, then slid his fingers into the hair at her nape, tilting her face up to his, daring her to ignore the electric leap of awareness that arced instantly between them. Gazes clashed, breaths shuddered, eternity faltered. Then he smiled and released her so abruptly she staggered, his low growl both a vow and a warning.

"We aren't done yet, darlin'. Not by a long shot."

"Now that's a load of bull."

"You said it, partner." Grinning, Travis watched two thousand pounds of Brahma come snorting and stomping down the loading chute and explode into the corral in a fit of ill-tempered bucking. The buff-colored bull cantered about, slinging his ferocious horns at imaginary foes, filling the sunny and unseasonably warm Tuesday morning with a flurry of red dust.

Sam Preston hooked a boot heel on the wooden fence and shoved his Stetson back on his sandy head. Angel

Morales, his cow boss, and a couple of relieved ranch hands latched the trailer's gate and drove the new truck rig, sporting the King and Preston Stock Company logo, toward the barn located behind the Preston ranch house. Between the Preston Lazy Diamond ranch and Travis's Flying K spread, a few miles south, King and Preston sported enough acreage to sustain a stock of Brahma and Corrientes cattle prime enough to tempt any rodeo supplier.

With Travis's capital and salesmanship skills and Sam's know-how and hands-on foremanship, they'd given their nearest competitor, Buzz Henry, a run for his money this year. Though things might still be a bit touch and go for the new company, Travis knew he'd made the smartest business decision of his career, throwing in with his best friend's older brother.

Now a grin that matched his partner's split Sam's craggy features. "Damn, that's a fine-lookin' animal. Rank and mean as hell by the looks of him, but that doesn't hurt when it comes to prime bucking stock."

"Yeah, this one looks like he was born mad, but ole Grenada ought to make himself a name on the circuit as well as sire a passel of bucking bulls for us."

"Thanks to your silver tongue and a knack for horse trading. Well done, hoss." Both men wore long-sleeved shirts and vests they didn't need, as the day warmed toward Indian Summer. Sam clapped Travis on the back, then frowned at his partner's wince of pain. "Hell, man. Don't tell me you got your chili cooled in Colorado Springs?"

Travis grimaced. "Let's just say I could have saved my plane fare."

"You all right?"

"What's another wreck? At least I didn't get hung up in the riggin' but once. I'll live. Hey, forget it."

Stoicism was a bull rider's stock in trade, but the fact was this past weekend he'd ridden like a rookie, never once making it to the whistle. A performance like that wouldn't get him far at the National Finals in Las Vegas in just over a month, and he'd been counting on taking the title again and winning some endorsements. A lucky man could make as much during the ten-day competition as he did all year long, and King and Preston needed the cash.

But besides empty pockets and battered pride, he'd ended up with more bruises that a porcupine had quills, his spine ached like the devil, and his leg was numb. If Mercy knew, she was sure to look down her patrician nose and say, "I told you so."

Hell, it was all her fault, anyway. Putting on her high-falutin' airs, turning him inside out with the power of her response to him and then denying it like the bald-faced liar she was, keeping him in such turmoil he didn't know which end of a bull was which. He knew better than to let a woman stir him up to the point he couldn't concentrate on his business.

It was dangerous. It was stupid. And he couldn't any more stop thinking about little Mercy Holt than he could stop breathing. But at least he could change the subject.

"The sheriff got anything on our missing stock?" he asked.

Sam shook his head as they sauntered toward the neat, white-painted ranch house. "Not a clue, dammit."

"That makes three head so far?"

"Four. Three out of the northeast pasture and one off of your place."

"Mine now, too? Hellfire!"

"Yup. Angel's having the hands keep a close eye out, much good it's done. Cut the fence, back up a trailer, and they're gone, hamburger in some galoot's skillet."

Travis groaned at the thought. Rodeo stock was too valuable to end up on the dinner table. "Geez, rustlers in this day and age. Sounds like vigilante time for you and me, partner."

"Sounds like you're right. We can't afford much more of this. Don't know why they'd single us out as a target, though."

"Best stock in the county, for one reason," Travis said.

Sam's mouth curled sourly. "Yeah, but whether it's some polecat looking for a way to pay off his bar tab or just a bunch of kids out on a lark or an organized ring of rustlers, it's still hitting us in the old pocketbook and it's got to stop. Only, the local constabulary can't come up with anything concrete to go on."

"Kids, huh?" Travis scowled and snapped his fingers. "Twice I've noticed some young kids hanging around where Hawkins Road turns off between my spread and the Turner place. Could have been up to no good."

Sam paused with a booted foot on the back step, his expression wry. "Speaking from experience, huh?"

"Well…" Travis winked. "Kenny and I pulled a stunt or two back in our time. Never stooped to rustling, though."

"You recognize any of these kids?"

"Naw. They took off in some kind of beat-up old truck before I got close enough, just like they were lookin' for trouble."

"Or running from it," Sam said, thoughtful. "Maybe the county juvenile officer might know something about them. What's her name—Jones?"

"Not Honey? Old Sally's red-haired granddaughter? Used to barrel race a little?"

"That's her. Doing a fine job with the youngsters hereabouts, too, by all accounts. Though I can't say much for her taste in boyfriends. That low-life she's been seeing is bad news."

"Well, why don't I just go see Honey this morning? Maybe she knows something about these boys."

"Good idea. It's a long shot, but the only lead so far." Sam opened the door, leading Travis into a homey country kitchen redolent with the scents of bacon and coffee. "But come on in and let Curly fix you up with some breakfast first."

"Your pretty wife has more to do than let a broken-down cowpoke mooch off her table."

"You know she's always had a soft spot for you."

Travis tossed his hat onto the peg beside Sam's and smoothed his mustache with a forefinger. "Never said the woman was smart—she married you, didn't she?"

"Best move he ever made," Roni Preston laughed from the doorway. The dark curls that fell over her sweater-clad shoulders were just as wild and unruly as the russet-colored locks sported by the toddler perched on her hip. She walked over and bussed Travis's cheek. "How you doing, handsome? Want some coffee?"

"Just fine, good-looking. And yeah, that'd be nice." Travis clapped his hands and reached for the baby. "Hey, Jessie, come see your Uncle Travis."

Jessie squealed and dimpled as Travis took her from her mother. Dropping into a kitchen chair, Travis bounced the little girl on his knee. He got quite a charge out of this kind of thing, thought he might even want a couple of ankle biters of his own someday. What startled him so much that he nearly bounced Jessie onto the floor was the realization that the faceless woman who'd been in his "someday" dreams had somehow taken on Mercy's features. It made him swallow hard.

Roni poured coffee, while Sam explained Travis's plan to see Honey Jones.

"Worth a try," Roni agreed. "And could you give me a lift to town? My truck's been in the shop and they just called to say it's ready."

"No problem." Travis grinned as Jessie patted his cheeks, then puckered up and gave him a sloppy kiss. "Uh-oh, Sam, I see big problems in your future—your daughter already likes kissing rodeo bums."

"I own a shotgun."

"If Sam has his way, she'll be an old maid," Roni said with a smile.

Sam crossed his arms, unrepentant. "I reckon running off smooth-talking caballeros is a dad's job. And since you've been run off a time or two yourself, Travis, what's this I hear about you squiring Mercedes Holt?"

Travis stiffened. "Just being friendly. I happened to be around when her dad had some sort of spell with his heart, so I gave her a ride into Flat Fork."

Roni smiled. "Krystal told me Doc Hazelton already kicked the judge out of the hospital, he's been such a bad patient."

Travis reached for his coffee cup. "I guess that's good news. Mercy ought to be happy."

"All I know is she sure led Kenny a merry dance," Sam said.

"That was a long time ago."

Curiosity flickered behind Sam's eyes at Travis's tone. "Wait a minute, are you telling me...?"

"Oh, hell, no!" Travis set his cup back down and

bounced Jessie a little faster. "Believe me, I never tried to horn in on my partner back then."

"But things change. She's a doctor herself now, isn't she? And it was a long time ago." Sam met Roni's inquisitive gaze and shrugged.

"Okay, spill it, Travis," Roni ordered. "What's going on?"

He blew out a silent breath of exasperation, then admitted, "Damned if I know."

Sam crossed his arms and leaned against the kitchen cabinet, his smile smug. "Well, well, well...never seen 'Love'em-and-leave'em' King in such a quandary."

"Don't start, Sam," Travis warned, pointing a finger. "I've busted better men for less."

Sam refused to take offense. "Hooee, this is serious."

"Don't let him rile you, Travis," Roni advised, scooping Jessie up with a tickle. "And don't worry. You know all the ladies love you."

Sure, Travis thought bleakly, all except the one who counts.

Four

Mercy dealt with trauma, death, mayhem. She handled distraught parents, hysterical children, psychotic criminals and arrogant doctors with cool aplomb on a nightly basis. So why, she asked herself, had managing one cantankerous patient for a mere five days put her on the verge of both mental and physical collapse?

Because it's Daddy, and you're still Daddy's little girl.

Mercy sighed and shifted the heavy manila folder she carried to a more comfortable position. Her heels clicked on the marble floor as she negotiated the busy courthouse's second floor. At least the Honorable Jonathan Holt's insistence that the Juvenile Task Force file could not be allowed to languish on his desk another minute had given her the excuse to leave the house, a break she welcomed.

While Jonathan's condition was improving, he wasn't exactly a model patient. In fact she'd practically bolted out of the door, ignoring the fact she looked like hell, clad in sloppy jeans and sweatshirt, bags under her eyes, hair screwed in a haphazard bun. Joycelyn would have been horrified if she'd seen her, but her mother had been taking a well-deserved nap, and Daisy, their housekeeper of many years, had been willing to listen for the judge's bell.

Mercy's lips twisted in a wry smile. She'd never thought that coming in to Flat Fork would give her so much pleasure. After she dropped off the packet, she might even take a moment to browse the pharmacy's book rack for something to entertain her father. And maybe after that she'd pick up a shake from the Tastee-Freeze, the double-chocolate deluxe kind she and Kenny and Travis used to love before everything changed, before she'd done the unforgivable, setting a course whose shadowy influences still lingered, unavoidable even after all this time.

Unwilling to pursue that unhappy train of thought, Mercy located the appropriate frosted-glass door, knocked, entered the little cubbyhole of an office and came up short.

A cinnamon-haired woman with a freckled, pixie face and shining green-gold eyes behind tortoiseshell glasses looked up from her cluttered desk. More disturbingly, Travis King lounged in the single, wooden chair beside the desk, his long legs outstretched, his coffee-brown eyes enigmatic.

"May I help you?" The young woman's bright smile radiated friendliness. She wore a deputy's uniform shirt with her khaki skirt, and Mercy realized that she was somewhat older than her youthful features suggested, certainly mature enough for the position of county juvenile officer.

"Ms. Jones? I've brought the judge's file—" She laid the bundle down on the desk.

"Of course. He just called. And I'm Honoria—Honey for short, Dr. Holt."

Mercy couldn't resist the other woman's congeniality. "And I've always been Mercy in these parts."

Honey beamed at her. "Great. This is perfect timing. You know Travis King, don't you?"

"Uh, yes." Mercy tucked a wayward strand of hair behind her ear, somewhat overwhelmed by Honey's enthusiastic response, not to mention Travis's unexpected presence.

Then he was climbing to his feet, and her gaze sharpened at the stiffness of his movements. He was hurt. Her eyes locked with his, and she knew instantly that his rodeoing in Colorado Springs the past weekend had cost him. She wanted to comfort his hurts and at the same time slap him silly for being such a jackass. Instead, she clamped her lips tight to keep from saying anything, only to be rewarded by the slight, mocking smile that appeared underneath his mustache.

We aren't done yet. The memory of that warning made her shiver.

Honey rattled merrily along, oblivious. "Travis just agreed to lend his name to publicize our barbecue next week."

"Barbecue?" Mercy echoed.

"Yes, and a big dance, too. A fund-raiser for the Juvenile Task Force." Her expression grew serious. "We've got some kids around here who deserve a break—summer camp, family counseling, that kind of thing. Money for these programs can help keep a good kid who's maybe headed down a bad track out of the courts. Tickets ought to go like hotcakes now that the world champion bull rider's involved.''

"Don't go getting your hopes up too high, darlin','' Travis drawled, hooking his thumbs in his belt loops. ''I'm just your average dumb cowpoke when you get down to it.''

Mercy felt a slow rise of heat stain her cheeks at his deliberate reference to their last conversation.

"Nonsense,'' Honey said. "You're way too modest. I know we'll have a rousing success with you on board. You'll tell the judge, won't you, Mercy? He'll be so pleased.''

"Uh, yes, I'll tell him. You say he called?'' Mercy shook her head. "That man. He's supposed to be resting.''

"He's doing okay, then?'' Travis asked quietly.

"Fairly well. He's impatient. It's going to take some time.''

"I don't envy you the task of convincing the judge about that,'' Honey said with a laugh. She flipped through a stack of papers and rose to her feet. "Look, I'll go down the hall and make a copy of this program for you to take it to him. He can look it over and give me any suggestions. Might occupy his mind for a time.''

"Thanks. That's a good idea,'' Mercy agreed.

"Be right back.''

The door slammed behind her, and there was a moment of awkward silence.

"You look plum worn out, darlin'.''

"How nice of you to notice—'' Mercy caught the sarcastic edge to her voice and broke off with a sigh. "Sorry, Travis. I don't know what makes me lash out like that. And I want to apologize for the other night. I said some things—'' She made a helpless gesture.

"We both did.''

"We're like oil and water, I guess. Just don't mix. So we shouldn't." She shrugged. "You understand it's better this way."

Gingerly he eased a hip onto the edge of the desk, and his eyes grew dark and fathomless as midnight. "For whom?"

She gulped. "For both of us."

"I'd say that's a matter of opinion."

In a man whose interest and devotion she deserved, such implacability and steadfast determination would have been thrilling indeed, but here it only filled her with dismay, because she knew the inevitable outcome would be disastrous. They had too much history and too many issues between them. Her only hope was to remove herself from the situation before the worst occurred. What that worst might be, she didn't want to contemplate.

"Travis—"

A curly head poked inside the door. "Hey, champ. You ready to go? Why, Mercy Holt, as I live and breathe."

"Roni Daniels. It's good to see you." Smiling, the two women hugged. They'd been acquaintances since girlhood, and since Roni had practically grown up with the Preston boys, she'd been around in the halcyon days of Mercy's crush on Kenny.

"It's Preston now," Roni laughed. "Can you believe it? Me and Sam."

"Congratulations. Travis told me the good news."

"Bragging, I expect," Roni teased. "Although he did have a little something to do with Sam Preston's seeing the error of his ways. Not the first time you ever played Cupid, huh, Travis?" Glancing at her watch, Roni missed Mercy's blush. "Listen, if we're going to get to the dealership before they close for lunch—"

"Right." He levered himself from the desk.

Honey breezed into the office, nodded to Roni and handed a sheaf of papers to Mercy. "Here you go."

"We'll have to get together for a real visit to catch up while you're here," Roni told Mercy, moving toward the door. "I'll call you, and we'll do something, okay?"

"Sure." Mercy nodded, knowing she had no intention of following through.

"And I certainly want you to attend the barbecue," Honey added. "You'll be the judge's official representative if he's not able to come."

Mercy carefully folded the papers and stuck them in her purse. "I'd like to, but I really can't commit to anything. I—I may not be around here that long."

"I thought you were staying through Thanksgiving," Travis said sharply. "Don't tell me they wouldn't give you a leave from that hospital of yours."

Actually, the administration had been quite accommodating, and extended leave had been easy to arrange, but she wasn't about to tell him that. Her mother was putting on enough pressure as it was without Travis adding to it. She made her voice purposefully cool and noncommittal.

"It's hard for me to make plans at this point, but of course I can't stay in Flat Fork indefinitely. You understand, don't you, Honey?"

The redhead looked disappointed, but nodded. "Just let me know if your plans change."

"We'd better hurry," Roni said. "See you, Mercy."

Travis followed. His eyes caught Mercy's, and as he passed, his rumbled comment was for her alone. "For a smart woman, you spend an awful lot of time avoiding the issue."

Mercy lifted her chin. "Meaning?"

"No matter how hard you try, darlin', you can't run forever."

Mercy took a last peek through her father's bedroom door, satisfied herself that he was sleeping peacefully, finally, after a difficult evening that had tried her patience and sent Joycelyn off to bed with a cold compress. Crossing the plushly carpeted upstairs corridor, Mercy let herself into her own room, her mother's idea of appropriate decor for the daughter of the most powerful man in the county, a feminine bower of lush rose-splashed wallpaper and cherry furniture that did nothing to soothe Mercy's overstretched nerves.

Thankfully, the only light came from a single, small Victorian lamp, allowing her to ignore the busy room. Restless, overstressed by Jonathan's impatience with his illness, Joycelyn's anxiety and her own mounting tension over what looked to be an extended stay in Flat Fork, she rubbed the knot in her aching neck. Crossing to the double window overlooking the side yard, she gazed avidly out into the Texas darkness like a prisoner offered a glimpse of freedom.

As badly as she hated to admit it, Travis was right, she did want to run away.

Her relationship with her parents had always alternated rebellion with acquiescence, and she was still trying to live up to their expectations, letting her own insecurities and guilt place her too often in the role of child, subject to all the manipulations of old programming. Though her folks were proud of her accomplishments, they were still faintly surprised at the path she'd chosen, had been more appalled by her decision to pursue medicine than by her divorce, in fact. It was simpler to maintain a healthy distance, although she regretted having to do so.

Unfortunately in the present situation that was impossible. That reality, coupled with leaving her job cold turkey and the emotional whirlwind of Travis storming her defenses, had her feeling as though she were trapped inside a pressure cooker with a faulty valve, ready to blow at any minute.

Mercy flattened her palm against the cool glass pane, frowning to herself. It had been the same as long as she could remember, the wildness building up inside her until the inevitable explosion occurred, luring her to actions and decisions she regretted. She'd had to wrestle hard with herself to gain control of those impulses, and she'd accomplished it with no little amount of heartache. But she considered that the cost of disciplining her spirit and spontaneity had been worth it.

And that was yet another reason why she refused to allow this thing with Travis to continue. He'd come closer than anyone in years to making her lose total control. Yes, she was running—running scared. Her victories had been too hard won to allow a moment of passion and pure insanity to pull her off the course she'd set for herself. Still, at moments like this, when the restlessness burned and she felt as wild as a mustang, it was damned hard to remember to be sensible.

Reaching for the lamp switch, she plunged the room into darkness, then reached for the hem of her sweatshirt. A tiny ping and rattle at the window startled her, and she paused, listening. A second click against the glass, the echo of a low whistle from below...

Old memories had her throwing up the sash and leaning out of the window. "Who's there?"

"Hello, darlin'."

The shadowy figure was nearly invisible despite a mercury security light that bathed the yard in pale lavender illumination, but the disembodied voice was like warm velvet, rippling sensation along her spine.

"Travis." How many times had he come to her like

this, carrying messages, shamelessly helping her sneak out to meet her boyfriend, simply sitting with her in the garage while she talked out her troubles to a friend with a sympathetic ear? She steeled herself against the wave of nostalgia, but couldn't keep her words from becoming a conspiratorial whisper, just like old times. "What do you want?"

"Can Mercy come out and play?"

His wheedling tone made her smile. She leaned her elbows against the sill. The cool wind held a breath of moisture and blew her hair into tendrils. "Are you nuts?"

"I ride bulls for a living, ma'am. What do you think?"

"You're certifiable."

"Then humor a lunatic. You said you won't be here much longer. Come visit with an old friend."

She knew better. Temptation waited below in tight black jeans. But she was feeling stifled, the offer more than she could resist with the pressure on her internal gauges at dangerous levels. Just for a little while, she promised herself. Just to remember old times. She reached for the wooden trellis attached to the side of the house, threw her leg over the windowsill in a movement that was still familiar after all these years, then shimmied down the rickety, ivy-encrusted structure.

"Mercy, what the hell—" With a muffled curse, Travis caught her as a support snapped and she nearly tumbled into the shrubbery. Beneath the shadow of his hat, his face was a study in starlit planes and angles, harsh with the fright she'd given him. Strong arms crushing her, he gave her a little shake.

"Lord, woman, I didn't mean that way. You could have broken your neck. You're too old for such foolishness."

Breathless at his nearness, feeling both triumphant and

recklessly euphoric, she shook her head. "Apparently not. And who gave you the monopoly on insane risks?"

"It's not the same."

She laughed. "The hell it's not. And keep your voice down. You'll wake the folks. Come on."

Taking his hand, she raced him across the grass down to the multicar garage that had once been a stable. Pulling him inside the dark structure, she released him, wandering past the dim hulks of the parked automobiles toward the end of the row where a tarp covered a vehicle she recognized.

"What are you doing here, Travis?"

"I don't know," he admitted, following her. "Maybe it's time to lay some ghosts to rest."

A shiver of panic coursed through her veins. No, she couldn't face that, not tonight. Reaching up, she yanked the chain attached to the single bulb, making them both blink at the sudden incandescence. With a flick of her wrist, she tugged the tarp free.

"Remember this?"

"Hard to forget." He stared at the still-bright paint of her old red Pontiac convertible. The top was down, the leather upholstery still supple, the chrome shiny. His lips curled underneath his mustache, but there was no humor in the smile. "Lots of memories in that back seat, huh, Mercy?"

His careless words took her breath, but she refused to let him see he'd wounded her with his assumptions. Setting her jaw, she opened the door and climbed in. The key was under the front seat as always, and when she started the ignition, the engine turned over without a protest, a testimony to the judge's conscientiousness. She turned on the headlights, then shot Travis a challenging look. "You coming?"

"Where?"

"Does it matter?" He looked uncertain, as if she'd spoken in some sort of alien language. Shrugging, she shifted into reverse. "Suit yourself."

"Wait up!" He hoisted himself over the door into the passenger seat.

Backing out of the garage, Mercy pointed the convertible into the night. Out on the main highway, she pressed the accelerator toward the floor and headed out of town.

The wind whipped her hair into a tangle and spanked her cheeks with cold, but she was too exhilarated, too liberated, to care. Freedom sang in her veins. The landscape flashed by, trees and pastures and fences passing in one dark blur of speed. She gripped the steering wheel, grinning, aware of Travis's growing scowl as he held on to the brim of his hat. Finally he grabbed her shoulder, shouting to be heard over the growl of the engine and scream of the wind.

"Slow this crate down! What the devil's gotten into you?"

"This is the real me, remember?" she shouted back. "The hellion. The wild woman."

"For God's sake—"

She stared through the windshield at the bands of light cutting a swath on the empty stretch of black asphalt. A tear-shaped drop splatted against the glass, then another. She didn't slow down. "I never slept with him."

"What?"

"Kenny and I, we didn't—"

A skittering flicker of movement—pointed snout, hard shell, long tail—Mercy twisted the wheel, tires skidding on the damp pavement as she dodged the armadillo foraging in the middle of the highway.

Braced against the dashboard, Travis roared a curse. "Slow down!"

She remembered, then, that he'd been the one at the wheel that awful night. Ashamed, contrite, she eased off the gas, pulled onto the grassy shoulder to park.

"I'm sorry." Shuddering, she reached blindly for him, clutching his shoulders as the cold rain began in earnest, pelting into her hair, running down her face to mingle with her tears. "Oh, God, Travis. I didn't mean to do that to you—"

"Sweet heaven, woman." She buried her face against his neck, trembling with remorse and reaction, and he groaned into her hair. "What is it? Tell me."

But how could she tell him what she didn't recognize or understand about herself at that moment?

She whispered against the stubble-rough curve of his lean jaw. "Just hold me."

His arms tightened around her, crushing her to his chest as if he could absorb the very essence of her. After a long moment, after the violence of her trembling had eased a trifle, he leaned back to peer into her face. "We're getting soaked."

"Yes."

Liquid dribbled off his hat brim, and his mouth quirked. "So's the car."

A gust of silent laughter caught Mercy by surprise. She licked the moisture from her lips. "Uh-huh. Must be a couple of damn fools sitting in it."

"Suppose we could put the top up."

"Try to beat eight seconds, cowboy."

Whooping, Mercy scrambled out of the car, unfastening latches, grabbing the black fold-over top, hurrying the mechanism while Travis hastily did the same on the passenger side. Silver sheets of rain hampered their efforts, soaked their clothes, turned Mercy's hair and Travis's mustache into drooping rat's tails.

Shrieking as the cold rain dripped down her spine, giggling at the disgruntled expression on Travis's face, Mercy gave in to hilarious laughter. Catching some of her manic contagion, Travis joined her in a flurry of curses and chuckles. The rag roof finally settled into place, and they dove back into the front seat, sliding on the wet leather, clutching at each other and holding their sides with an explosion of hilarity.

"Neither of us—" Mercy gasped "—have sense enough…"

"…to come in out of the rain," he finished.

Travis sluiced moisture from his face and mustache, grinning. Mercy leaned her head back, trying to catch her breath.

His smile softened, and he whisked his knuckles down her damp cheek. "It's good to hear you laugh, darlin'."

"It feels good."

The rain beat a tattoo on the cloth top and obscured the windows, insulating them from the outside world in an intimate cocoon. She gazed up at him through sodden tendrils, weak from the release of tension, not even caring that her smile was sappy. The silliness, the fun—how she'd missed it, and how she envied Travis for his capacity to enjoy it. Looking into his mischievous brown eyes, she wished…

Before she could finish the thought, a tremendous chill shook her.

Travis frowned. "Okay, scoot over."

"What? Hey." He plopped her into the passenger seat and slid behind the wheel. "What's the meaning of this, cowboy?"

"It means I'll be damned if you're catching pneumonia

on my time. So relax, doctor, the cavalry's on its way, and this time, *I'm* driving.''

Travis tossed another stick into the native stone fire-place, hooked a thumb into his belt loop and stared at the orange flames licking at the kindling he'd lit. A damp towel hung around his naked shoulders and his feet were bare, but at least his jeans were dry. He cast a glance down the hall leading to the bath where Mercy was chang-ing. The modest Flying K ranch house didn't boast the amenities of the Holt mansion, but they'd only been a mile from the entrance gate, and dry things had been the only order of business on his mind after that wild ride.

No, that was a lie. What he couldn't get out of his head was that soft confession of hers. She and Kenny hadn't been lovers. After all this time, it shouldn't matter. It did, shamefully.

Jealousy, guilt, covetousness—they weren't things a man was proud to find within himself. And heck, it wasn't as if her admission made any real difference. Mercy had been married, for God's sake! And as for his own rela-tionships, there were too many women already under that bridge. Still, something deep and primal resonated with satisfaction, knowing that she and Kenny hadn't been in-timate. He wondered why not.

"I'm glad to see you own at least one article of clothing that isn't black."

Travis swung around, then swallowed hard. The old plaid flannel shirt Mercy wore hung over her fingertips and modestly dropped to her kneecaps. It also clung to every line and curve of her body, soft and sinuous and revealing as a second skin. She'd pulled on a pair of his white athletic socks and combed her damp hair into order behind her ears, but that didn't spoil the effect the sight of her was having on his libido. He cleared his throat with difficulty.

"I come out of costume occasionally. Glad you approve."

"I put the wet things in your dryer. Is that okay?" She drifted toward the fire, silent as a cat on her sock feet as she came up beside him. He caught a whiff of his own shampoo, the scent on her changed into something gut-tighteningly feminine.

"Sure. Your lips are still blue. Want a brandy or something to warm you up?"

Her gaze flicked to the mug he'd set on the carved oak mantel. "Whatever you're having is fine."

"Hot chocolate."

Her lips twisted. "You really know how to live it up, don't you, cowboy?"

"I gave up the hard stuff a long time ago." They both knew why. She caught his eye, then glanced away. "Here," he said, "take this."

"Oh, but—"

He pressed the mug into her hands, cupping her cool fingers around the warm ceramic, his skin tingling from the contact as if from an electrical surge. "I'll pour myself another," he said gruffly.

Bluebonnet eyes watchful over the rim of the mug, she sipped the creamy concoction, then licked the foam from her upper lip with the tip of her tongue. The bottom fell out of Travis's belly. God, was she being purposefully provocative, or was he simply so hungry for her that every gesture, every movement seemed designed to drive him completely around the bend?

Looking around the masculine den, Mercy pressed the cup against the middle of her chest, warming herself, warming Travis with the way the movement pressed flannel against lush curves. "You have a nice place."

"It suits me." The brass-trimmed green leather couches and heavy-duty armchairs fit a man's demands for comfort, the spartan decor a sense of order and stability. Not that a woman's touch wouldn't be welcome, he thought, if she were the right woman. "Don't get to spend as much time here as I like, of course."

She gave a little snort. "No great loss. What's in Flat Fork, anyway?"

"Home. God-fearing, hard-working folks. Space to feel free." He gripped the edges of his towel, frowning slightly. "I depend on Sam and the hands to run the Flying K while I'm on the circuit, but I even miss the day-to-day cowboying. Plus the fun of chasing rustlers."

"Rustlers?"

"Yeah, some of our best stock's gone missing recently. Maybe kids." He shrugged. "I was trying to get a handle on it with Honey this morning."

A touch of acid laced her voice. "So there's trouble in paradise after all."

"Admit it, this wasn't such a bad place to grow up. It still isn't."

She tossed her head, flippant. "As Einstein said, everything's relative."

"It'd be a good place to raise a family." Her startled look caught him off guard. "You know, two-point-five kids and a dog? Ever thought about it, Mercy?"

"No." Her voice was flat. She thrust her mug at him, a reckless light rekindling in her eyes. "How about a refill, cowboy? I feel like living dangerously tonight."

"Drowning your sorrows? Trust me. It doesn't work." He took the cup from her nerveless fingers and turned away. "I'll get that chocolate."

She gave a sharp cry that froze him in his tracks. Before he could turn around again she was at his back, plucking the towel from his shoulders, her hands pressing at the black and blue place on his left side.

"Good Lord, is this what you did in Colorado Springs?"

He went poker stiff, staring straight ahead into the fire, his jaw clenched. "Besides humiliating myself, you mean? Yeah."

"What happened?" She palpated the sore flesh, evoking a wince he couldn't hide.

"Rode like a greenhorn, that's all. Had things on my mind."

"You could have ruptured your kidney."

Her words were angry, but her touch was a sweet agony that made his voice rasp in his throat like the woodsmoke rising up the chimney. "I'm all right."

"No blood? What about—"

"Dammit!" Whirling, he caught her wrists and pinioned them against his hair-dusted chest. "I said I'm fine."

Her eyes widened at the sight of the livid scrape running from his collarbone to his waistband. Captive, she tilted her chin and glared at him. "Besides being a damned fool, you're a liar, cowboy."

"Spare me the lecture, Doc," he growled. "Your bedside manner stinks."

"I'll see what I can do about it." With a feline smile, she swayed toward him, brushing her lips across the angry welt.

He jumped as if burned. "What the *hell* are you doing?"

"Kissing you better."

This time when her mouth touched his chest, he felt

her wet tongue flick against his flesh, and lightning jolted through his veins, lodging in his loins in an urgency of need that had him cursing.

"Damnation, woman, you'd better know what kind of game you're playing."

Struggling to break his grip on her wrists, her breathing ragged, she surged upward on her tiptoes, boldly capturing his mouth with hers. "Just...shut up."

Then she kissed him again.

Groaning, Travis released her wrists, clamped his arms around her and pulled her into the cradle of his thighs, letting her feel exactly what her provocation had done to him. Linking her arms around his neck, she opened her mouth fully to his invading tongue and wiggled voluptuously, sliding soft flannel and softer woman beneath it against the rough denim strained against his arousal.

She tasted sweetly of chocolate and woman. Sculpting her curves with his palms, he explored her, pressing her closer. She responded with a wildness that electrified him, nipping at his lips, aggressively tracing the ripple of muscle over his belly with her fingertips into the dip of his waistband. Travis slipped his hands to her slim thighs, rode the satiny skin upward beneath the hem of the shirt, finding to his shock that she was naked beneath the garment. Fingers kneading her flesh, he ground her against himself, evoking mutual moans of need.

Heart pounding, his breath a razor in his chest, Travis drew back to look at her. Her hair was drying in a glorious halo about her face, and her eyes burned bright—almost too bright. Watching him, she smiled—a smile full of daring and reckless challenge—then unfastened the first button on her shirt.

It didn't ring true. Her words came back to him... "living dangerously tonight."

It hit him then with all the devastating force of a raging Brahma. The manic mood of hers was something out of the past, a conjuring of the old Mercy, the one who shimmied down trellises and drove her convertible with the fearlessness of a madwoman. And any decision this Mercy made tonight couldn't be trusted, because on the morrow she'd have vanished into the distant past again, leaving behind a woman whose regrets would be insurmountable.

And who would she blame the morning after? The blockheaded bull rider who'd taken advantage of her weakness. Cursing inwardly, he knew he couldn't risk it. Not if he wanted more from her than a single night. And, God help him, he did, much more.

Biting back a groan of pure frustration, his body screaming in protest at the very idea of what he was about to do, Travis folded his hands around Mercy's as she reached for the second button.

"That's enough."

"Hmm?" Puzzlement changed to understanding, and she gave him a pouty smile. "Like to do it yourself, do you, cowboy? Be my guest."

"Stop it." Deliberately he refastened the top button. "This has gone far enough."

She looked as though she'd been poleaxed, then a scarlet flood stained her cheeks. Jerking free of his hold, she glared at him, her eyes burning with fury and hurt. "Well, excuse me. I could have sworn this is what you've been after all along."

"Not like this." He rubbed his nape in exasperation, knowing he was making a mishmash of things.

"What, you mean on my terms instead of just yours?" She gave a harsh laugh. "Typical. What's the matter, cowboy, afraid you can't handle a real woman?"

"The mood you're in, you're not thinking straight."

She drew in a hiss of pure outrage. "Who are you to make that kind of judgment for me? I won't be treated like a dim-witted child."

"Then don't act like one by throwing a tantrum when you don't get your way. I'm trying to do what's best here."

"Pardon me if I question this sudden burst of nobility in a man who's been making every effort to get into my panties," she said with a sneer.

Travis's temper snapped, and he grabbed her upper arms. "Look, you know I want you so bad I'm crazy with it, but if it happens—*when* it happens between us—I don't want you to have any regrets. That's all it would be tonight, and if you don't know it now, you'll know it soon enough."

She went absolutely still, the hellion replaced by the ice maiden, her voice frigid with scorn. "What I know, cowboy, is that it'll be a cold day in hell before I ever let you touch me again."

Five

"You look like somethin' the cat dragged in."

"Thank you, Daisy. You always did know how to flatter a gal's ego."

With a tired sigh, Mercy threw her keys and bag into the middle of the breakfast table and flopped into one of the heavy bow-backed chairs. The stocky, gray-haired housekeeper's assessment wasn't far off the mark, considering the rumpled jeans and plaid man's shirt she still wore, not to mention the sleepless night she'd just spent prowling the county highways until dawn in a vain effort to answer the question of the hour: what makes Mercy run?

Threading her fingers through her hair, she planted her elbows on the table and sniffed the coffee-flavored air appreciatively. "Want some help with breakfast?"

Daisy paused over the orange halves she was squeezing into a crystal pitcher, the look on her sun-weathered face incredulous. "You? Miss Useless? The day I turn you loose in my kitchen—despite the glass-and-tile monstrosity your mother's made of it—is the day I hang up my apron."

"You know, if you'd given me half a chance as a kid, maybe I wouldn't be all thumbs behind a stove now," Mercy replied mildly.

Daisy snorted. "And when did you ever show any interest in such things, I might ask? Social butterfly, belle of the county, cavorting with all sorts of riffraff all the livelong day and night...."

"Which, unfortunately, still seems to be the case." Dressed in an azure sweater dress, Joycelyn stood in the kitchen doorway, rubbing the last of her skin lotion into her slim, beringed hands. The storm had blown in a cold front along with a plenitude of sunshine, and the morning light streaming in the banks of kitchen windows clearly showed an expression pinched with reproof as she gazed at her only daughter.

Mercy stifled a grimace. "Good morning to you, too, Mother."

"I don't know how you can look me in the eye and say that, after what you've been doing all night."

Rising, Mercy helped herself to a cup of coffee from the pot on the counter. Fatigue and lack of sleep gave her a clarity of thought that might otherwise have been lacking. It occurred to her that although her parents would never change, that didn't mean she couldn't alter her own reactions, stop the cycle of guilt and blame, and perhaps shape how they perceived her into a new image.

Rather than rising to the bait in anger, she concentrated on keeping her voice calm. "Oh? And what have I been doing?"

"I think it's distressingly obvious." Joycelyn's gaze

narrowed on the plaid shirt with distaste. "You haven't outgrown your unfortunate predilection for rodeo men."

True enough, Mercy had to agree, but after Travis's rejection, she thought she was well on her way toward getting over that. Sometime between first light and break of day, somewhere fifty miles from nowhere, she'd come to the realization that she ought to be grateful he'd called a halt to things, whatever his cockeyed reasoning.

At the time, making love with Travis had seemed perfectly rational. Maybe after all the sexual buildup he'd been supplying she'd simply needed to get it over with, to put it behind her so she could move on when she left Flat Fork. And maybe she'd just *wanted*. Was that so hard to believe—that she had needs, that she longed for a tender touch like other women? God knew she'd relegated those urges to the back burner for longer than she cared to think about.

Nevertheless she was disgruntled to admit he'd been right. A smart woman had no business playing with fire, and Travis King was a conflagration. So no regrets, as he'd said. Except her secret one, well hidden, that they hadn't made love. And now they never would.

"Well?" her mother demanded. "What have you got to say for yourself?"

"Do we have to have this conversation?"

"Your conduct continues to disappoint me, Mercedes. I don't ask for much, but behaving in such a shameless manner while at this very minute your father needs you—"

"I've already checked on Daddy. His blood pressure's okay, and I drew the blood for the lab tests I ordered." Striving for composure, Mercy nodded to Daisy. "He's chomping at the bit for his orange juice, by the way."

"I'm going, I'm going." Muttering under her breath,

Daisy slammed a tumbler and the pitcher of juice onto a silver tray and stomped off toward the staircase.

Joycelyn marched to the coffeepot and poured herself a cup. "I suppose you slept with him?"

Mercy stiffened. "The fact that I'm a medical doctor held in high esteem by my colleagues, as well as a full-grown woman with a right to her privacy has no bearing on anything, I guess?"

"I think I have a right to know if my daughter's latest exploits are going to be the hottest gossip in town." Exasperation laced her voice. "For God's sake, Mercedes! Think of your father's position. At least I hope you were discreet. And if you must indulge in some sordid little affair, couldn't you choose someone more..."

Anger began to simmer, and Mercy's eyes narrowed. "More what?"

"More our own kind, with a similar standing in the community."

"Like my socially acceptable ex-husband, the adulterous worm, for instance?"

Joycelyn gave a little huff of annoyance. "Really, must you be so crass?"

Mercy felt a knot throb in the back of her neck, and all her good intentions almost flew out the window. How would her mother feel if she learned Travis had turned Mercy down. For a moment she battled a rebellious impulse to blurt out the truth. Luckily, the telephone saved the day as it clanged on the wall. Grateful for the reprieve from Joycelyn's accusations, Mercy grabbed the receiver. "Oh, hello, Roni. No, I've been up. Yes, I guess a baby does start your day off bright and early. What's that? Friday night at Rosie's with you and Sam? Uh..."

She hesitated, twirling the cord around her finger as she recalled her earlier reservations, why reconnecting to life

in Flat Fork on any level wasn't a good idea. Then she
looked up to find her mother frowning with disapproval—
of Mercy's friends, her choices, her life.

"Thank you, Roni," she said sweetly. "I'd love to."

On Friday night the steaks at Rosie's Café were rare,
the longnecks cold, the country-western music boisterous
and Roni and Sam Prestons' company surprisingly un-
complicated. In fact, the conversation was so general,
passing quickly over the two sticky subjects—Travis and
Kenny—that Mercy had dreaded most, that she found herself truly relaxing and actually enjoying herself for the
first time since coming home. So later, when Sam insisted
the best way to finish out an autumn evening was to drop
in on the local high school football game, Mercy could
only blame her full stomach and mellow mood for her
foolhardiness.

"I see the folks in Flat Fork still take their football
seriously."

Mercy surveyed the avid crowd overflowing the concrete and steel pipe bleachers, waving pennants and Texas
flags, ringing cowbells and cheering as the teams surged
up and down the playing field. The air was clear and crisp
enough to redden noses and make her glad of her tweed
jacket and slacks and navy cowl-necked sweater. The aro-
mas of buttered popcorn and burgers sizzling over char-
coal wafted upward on the breeze from the refreshment
booth. A large banner that said Mustangs Take State
draped the tin-roofed press box at the top of the stands,
and a deep-voiced announcer called out play-by-play over
the loudspeakers.

"Damn straight we do." Sam grinned and handed tickets to the teenaged attendant, then started up the bleacher
steps.

"Especially the semifinal playoff game," Roni added, tucking her hands into her melton car coat as she and Mercy followed. "It doesn't get any bigger than this in Flat Fork tonight."

Mercy had to smile in agreement. They found seats on the center aisle halfway up the stands, the Prestons answering greetings from neighbors, nodding to acquaintances, welcomed by a general aura of community and camaraderie that made Mercy feel a little lost. With a host of curious eyes on her, she barely resisted a nervous need to check her loose topknot and gold hoop earrings, sliding gratefully onto the outside aisle seat beside Roni.

"If the Mustangs win tonight, you'll have to come cheer for them in the finals," Roni said cheerfully. "Think you'll be around town next week?"

"Probably," Mercy admitted. "At least through Thanksgiving. Although Mother and I crank along like broken gears sometimes, my being here is taking the pressure off where Daddy's concerned. I have to admit I'm going a little stir crazy missing the E.R. madhouse, though."

"I'm sure Doc Hazelton could find you something to do to keep you out of trouble." Roni's eyes danced with mischief and a hint of calculation. "He's getting on, you know. He deserves to begin to take it easier, and this town sure could use another doctor."

"What are you plotting over there, Curly?" Sam asked, draping an affectionate hand over her knee.

"Oh, nothing," she said airily. "Just planting a seed."

Sam grinned under his Stetson. "Subtle she's not."

Mercy laughed wryly. "I'm flattered by the suggestion, but I'm quite happy where I am."

If you like nonstop work, no social life, no strings.
Mercy frowned at the inner voice, willing it to silence.

She was perfectly content, and no one could tell her otherwise.

"Well, it was just a thought—oh, *go!*" Roni surged to her feet, joining the cheering crowd as a Mustang running back broke out of a tackle for a big gain. Overhead, the announcer drawled names, downs and yards to go in a velvet voice that feathered a familiar tickle down Mercy's spine.

As Sam and Roni sat back down, Mercy cocked an ear. "Good Lord, is that—?"

Roni nodded. "Uh-huh, Travis. Guess Mr. Kaplan still has the flu. They get Travis to pinch hit whenever he's in town. He's pretty good at all that palaver, isn't he?"

Mercy's tone went dry. "Yes, he definitely has a way with sweet talk."

"I'll say. A cable sports channel wanted him to do some commentary a while back for them, but his being on the circuit made it hard to schedule."

"I thought he rodeoed every weekend," Mercy said.

Eyes on the next play, Sam gave a brief nod. "Just about. Makes one a weekend this time of year, one a day in summer for about a hundred-twenty rodeos a year, average. He's laying out this weekend to heal up for the last couple before the Las Vegas finals."

Knowing Travis's physical condition, Mercy felt a tingle of dread. If he'd made this concession to his ailments, was his condition worse than she feared?

"Think he'll win it all again, Sam?" Roni asked.

"The man knows what he's doing on a bull better'n anybody in the business, because he loves it. The smell of the rosin, the bull rope bell a-clangin', pitting himself against pure brute power and coming out on top. All he's got to do is draw a couple of real snot-slingers—"

"You mean animals rank enough to kill him," Mercy said sharply.

Sam shot her a curious look. "Or run up his scores. That's part of the risk, Mercy. You can't ride the pups to the big money. You know that."

"Sorry." She shrugged and tried to smile. "Mayhem and blood are my business, and I see quite enough accidently spilled without feeling I have to condone a man who courts destruction with his eyes open."

"It's his choice."

"Yes." Her mouth set. "It is that."

Boots clattered on the steps, then a lean figure in black scooted onto the metal seat beside Mercy. "Howdy."

She gasped and glared at Travis, caught between his hard length and Roni. "What the devil—?"

"Hold that thought, darlin'." He winked and grinned, then leaned over her lap to punch Sam and point down at the entrance aisle of the grandstands. "Look'er there, partner. See that kid giving Honey a hard time?"

The cinnamon-haired juvenile officer stood at the railing below them locked in a low-voiced, nose-to-nose confrontation with a wiry, black-eyed boy of about thirteen. His sullen expression and insolent stance was more proof than words of what he thought about the lecture. A trio of older teenage boys watched from a few feet back, cigarettes dangling in James Dean fashion, egging the younger kid on with their comments.

Sam nodded. "Yeah, what about him?"

"Damned if he's not one of those punks I saw hanging out around my place."

"That's Chase Conly," Roni said, frowning. "I think he lives out your way with an uncle or somebody."

Honey didn't seem to be making any headway. The boy scowled and went to turn away. Honey caught his shirt-front to stop him, and he knocked her hand aside, then stormed off, joining his jeering companions and leaving her red-faced with frustration.

"I've got to get back to the press box," Travis said. "Think you could maybe see what this kid's up to, Sam?"

Sam's jaw tightened, and he rose. "Might not be a bad idea. Excuse me, ladies."

Travis stood to let him out, then bent down and whispered in Mercy's ear. "You look like a million bucks tonight, darlin'."

Mercy gave him a cool look. "Save the sweet talk for someone who appreciates it, cowboy."

A shadow crossed behind his eyes, but his mustache quirked with his usual teasing banter. "Back to square one, are we?"

"Less than that."

Never one to ignore a challenge, he gave her a slow smile that riled her temper while it melted her insides. "Well, darlin', as the old hound dog says, there's more than one way to skin a cat."

Taking the steps two at a time—to prove that he wasn't half crippled, no matter how it hurt him, Mercy thought sourly—Travis made his way back to the press box.

Roni brushed her dark curls over her shoulders and gave Mercy a knowing look. "Like that, is it?"

"No. Not at all."

"I always wondered...I mean, I know you were crazy about Kenny, but there was something back then—"

"Cut it out. You're imagining things." Mercy hoped the cold air could account for her pink cheeks.

Roni looked dubious. "Well, if you say so—"

"Touchdown!" boomed from the loudspeakers.

The home crowd went crazy. The band awaiting halftime on the edges of the field struck up a victory march. Everyone hugged and shouted as Travis described the action, the extra point attempt, the last few seconds of the half. Even Mercy felt the euphoria, smiling at Roni as everyone settled back down in their seats.

"...and that's the Mustangs, leading fourteen to six as we end the half, ladies and gentlemen," Travis said, his deep tones reverberating over the noisy stands. "Before we start the halftime festivities, we've got to tend to some business. First order of which is a big hometown welcome for a former Flat Fork High homecoming queen—Ms. Mercedes Holt. Stand up there, Mercy, and wave howdy to the folks."

Mercy gulped and her face flamed in embarrassment. "Oh, that sorry—"

Giggling, Roni poked her. "Go ahead, get up."

What else could she do? Rising, Mercy plastered her best "Miss Flat Fork" smile on her face and raised a hand to acknowledge the warm applause from the crowd. Shooting a look that was pure daggers toward the dark figure holding a mike inside the press box, she sat down as quickly as possible, muttering dire threats under her breath.

Travis's monologue continued undeterred.

"Now, everyone knows Mercy's dad, our own Judge Jonathan Holt, has been a bit under the weather—glad to say he's doing better—but he's got a big Texas invitation for everyone to attend the Juvenile Task Force barbecue and dance next week. Look here, folks. The task force needs the money, and it's gonna be a whale of a good party. There's Ms. Honey Jones at the fence waiting to sell you a ticket. Say howdy, Honey."

"Howdy." Apparently recovered from her confrontation with Chase Conly, the pixie-faced lady at the railing grinned and held up double handfuls of printed tickets. "Come and get 'em."

"That's it, march right down, folks," Travis cajoled over the speakers. "Don't be cheapskates. Your neighbors are watching, and it's for a great cause."

Roni was laughing outright, watching the ticket buyers swarm Honey. "He's absolutely shameless, isn't he?"

"Among other things," Mercy said darkly.

"Come on. Cowboy up! Can't get the halftime show started until Honey sells out." Travis stood in the press box door, gesturing to the crowd to hurry with his microphone.

"Hey, Travis," someone shouted. "What about your tickets?"

Under his black hat, Travis's dark eyes gleamed and he pulled a pair from his shirt pocket, waving them overhead. "Already got 'em, Buck. Proud to say I'll have the very great pleasure of escorting the beautiful Mercy Holt as the judge's official representative that night."

"What!" Gasping, Mercy pivoted in her seat and glared at the figure at the top of the bleachers. "I never—"

"Miss Mercy is a doctor in the fine city of Ft. Worth nowadays," Travis continued, "so maybe we can't talk her into the kissing booth like she did in high school, but Dr. Holt can still take—or is that raise?—your blood pressure. So come join us. You'll be glad you did. Now, on with the halftime show...."

The throng laughed and applauded, several acquaintances calling approval and good-natured encouragement to Mercy. Folks heading for the snack stand patted her on the shoulder as they passed. If she hadn't been quite so chagrined, she might have enjoyed the feelings of acceptance more, would have basked in the warm glow of pride in one of their own that was radiated by her fellow towns-people, could have discovered that it canceled out some of the old negatives conjured by her own attitude toward Flat Fork and its inhabitants. As it was, she knew she'd have to explore those feelings another time.

Forced to smile and accept the well-meaning congrat-ulations and praise of friends and neighbors, she barely resisted the urge to denounce Travis as a conniving, lying scoundrel. But she was still trapped by other people's ex-pectations, and to refuse to appear at such a worthy com-munity cause would only make her look small and mean spirited.

So she gritted her teeth and plotted vengeance. Travis King had backed her into one too many corners. He'd gone too far, and he was going to pay, big-time.

Travis knew Mercy was going to make him pay. He just didn't know how yet. Or when. And waiting for the other boot to drop made him as jumpy as a bit-up old bull in fly time.

As the judge crossed the marble foyer of the Holt man-sion the night of the barbecue, Travis figured maybe the first gauntlet Mercy had thrown down for him was to face her pa.

"Travis, my boy, come on in." Jonathan stretched out his hand to shake, then clapped Travis on the back and urged him toward the richly appointed living room. He looked a bit thin in slacks and lumberjack plaid shirt, but his color was ruddy and the smile that had won him many an election was still firmly in place. "Mercy ought to be ready in a minute."

"Glad to see you looking so well, Your Honor." Travis cleared his throat, trying not to act like a green kid on his first date.

Jonathan dropped into an uncomfortable-looking mahogany and brocade chair and waved Travis toward another. "Damn quacks, all of 'em, and that includes my daughter. I'm feeling fine, and they still won't let me go back to work."

"I know just how you feel," Travis said, his mouth wry. Hat in his hand, he perched gingerly on the edge of the chair, wincing as it creaked under his weight.

At one time he would have been thoroughly intimidated by the opulence of the room with its crystal chandeliers and European antiques, but he'd seen and done a few things, rubbed elbows with high-powered promoters, held his own with some of society's best in places like Denver and Los Angeles. He might have gotten his basic education in the school of hard knocks, but life had smoothed some of his rough edges. To give the judge credit, he had the common touch, and although the man might have reservations about a rodeo bum and his only daughter, Travis felt a certain rapport that he knew was shared.

"Been out of the loop a time or two myself," Travis confided. "Makes a man antsy as hell."

"You ain't just whistling 'Dixie.' So I'm mighty grateful for the way you've pitched in with this fund-raiser, son. It's a pet project of mine, and I hate to miss out on it, but with you and Mercy helping Honey Jones, I know everything's in good hands."

"My pleasure, sir. Like to give the kids around here a chance. Fact is, time was I had my own share of teenage problems. If it hadn't been for rodeoing—" He shrugged.

The judge laughed, but there was respect in his regard. "Yes, sir, and now you're the world champion and a successful businessman, and my little girl's a dad-gum doctor. She even gave Doc Hazelton a hand at his clinic a time or two this past week. Who could have guessed, back when you wild kids were giving us all gray hair, that you'd come this far? Makes me proud of what we've raised up here in Flat Fork."

"Why, Daddy, I think that's the first time I've ever heard you say that." Pleasure, bemusement and surprise flavored Mercy's quiet statement from the doorway.

She glided into the room, and Travis rose to his feet. Her hair fell in honey gold curls to her shoulders, and she wore a tiered Western skirt in tones of teal and purple that made her eyes look violet, matching shirt, boots and Western belt buckle. Navajo silver jewelry graced her ears and throat. A stethoscope was draped incongruously around her neck, and she carried a blood pressure cuff. It was the first time he'd seen her since the football game, and she stole his breath.

"Just because a man doesn't say it, doesn't mean it's not the way he feels," Jonathan said grumpily.

"It's still nice to hear," she said, bending to buss his cheek. "Thank you." She went to work with the cuff, asking pleasantly, "How are you tonight, Travis?"

"Uh...just fine, darlin'."

"Be with you in a moment." She inserted the earpieces and frowned in concentration.

"Take your time." Mouth dry, Travis tried to still the flare of hunger merely looking at her ignited. Apparently she'd had time to cool off about the way he'd manipulated her into this. Maybe he'd get through the evening with his hide intact. And maybe he could use the opportunity to rebuild some bridges that had been burned.

"Quit your fretting, Mercy," the judge ordered. "You'll be late."

"I'm sure they'll save some barbecue for us." Satisfied, she refolded the cuff, then gave her father a stern look. "You'll take your medication?"

"You don't have to lecture me like I was six. Your mother won't let me forget." Jonathan waved at them. "Now git. And have a good time."

"I'm sure we will," she murmured, then smiled at Travis. "Ready?"

Bidding the judge goodbye, Travis helped her with her coat, then led her outside to his waiting truck. As they drove, her pleasantries about the crisp weather, the brilliance of the stars and how she was looking forward to eating real Texas barbecue made him more and more uneasy. He finally decided to take the proverbial bull by the horns.

"You don't have to pretend you aren't mad about this," he said as he found a spot for the truck in the jammed lot at the VFW hall.

Pockets of party-goers milled around all over the gravel lot, spilled out the hall's brightly lit doorways, came and went at the entrance. Cooks attended the three mobile barbecue pits set up on the side of the building, and the aromatic smoke of charring meat and tomato sauce filled the air with a pungency that made bellies growl and noses sniff appreciatively. The twangy sounds of a country band filtered into the night.

"Go ahead," he said, "lay into me and get it over with. We'll both feel better."

"I'm sure we're both adult enough to put aside our differences to benefit a worthy cause." Her eyes were calm and guileless. "Let's go inside. I'm starved."

The mildness of her answer did nothing to assuage his suspicions. Still, he'd have been a fool not to take what advantage he could of her unexpected agreeableness, so he turned on the charm. If she really was in a forgiving mood, maybe they could get past this rocky place in their relationship and start over.

Loading plates with ribs and chicken, saucy baked beans and potato salad, they headed for one of the many paper-covered tables to eat and visit with Sam and Roni and Roni's best friend, Kyrstal Harrison, and her husband, Bud. Honey was in evidence everywhere, flitting like a bee from bandstand to kitchen and back, making certain that everything ran smoothly.

After the meal, they all joined the dancers circling the floor, and Travis found that despite her protests Mercy hadn't forgotten the Texas Swing or the two-step. He wasn't exactly thrilled that a host of friends, and especially the single men of the community, kept cutting in on them, but it was clear that Mercy was doing her best public relations work for her father's project, cajoling her partners to drop a ten or twenty into the fishbowl Honey had set up for donations.

It still made him jealous as hell.

He finally reclaimed her for a waltz, nearly groaning with the pleasure of fitting her close to him, twirling in time to the music and breathing in the flowery scent of her hair. Despite the serenity she'd projected all evening, he felt the way her fingers trembled in his grasp, and she didn't turn away when he pressed his cheek next to hers, merely sighed softly and floated in his arms. Desire and longing and utter need filled his chest. She was driving him nuts.

The band's lead singer crooned about lost loves and past mistakes. Travis's voice was thick in his own ears. "Mercy—"

"Hmm?"

"Could we get out of here?"

"Why?"

"We need to talk."

"We'll just end up fighting again."

He drew back a little, but her eyes were downcast, her lashes lush against the pink-and-white perfection of her skin. He couldn't read her expression. "No, I promise—"

Honey appeared through the slow-moving stream of dancers, smiling cheerfully. "Almost time, Mercy."

"Thanks." Mercy nodded, but the other woman had already buzzed off again.

"Time for what?" Travis asked.

"To auction off a few things to raise more money. You'll help, won't you?"

Just when he'd been hoping to make a quick escape with Mercy. Biting back a curse of frustration, he nodded. "Sure, darlin', as long as we can keep on dancing."

Raising her eyes, she gave him a soft smile that launched his heart into orbit. "I knew I could count on you."

"Always." He swallowed, words of confession and longing filling his throat. "Darlin', we—" He broke off with a growl as Sam walked up and tapped him on the shoulder. The other dancers flowed around them as he glared at his friend. "Don't even think it, partner. I just got my hands back on the lady, and I'm not letting go for you or any other cowpuncher."

"Understandable." Sam's lips twisted in a brief smile for Mercy, but then his jaw tightened. "But it ain't that. Angel just called. Damned if we haven't lost four more steers, and this time they even went after Grenada."

"What!" Travis bit out a string of curses. Mercy frowned as Sam continued.

"Couldn't handle him, evidently. Angel says he's run through two fences. I'm going to get the sheriff on it and go give Angel a hand."

"I'll come with you."

"Naw, I can handle it." Sam jerked his head toward

the bandstand where Honey was announcing the totals raised for the night and calling for Travis to come up front. "This is sort of your shindig. Better see it out. I'll let you know when I find out anything."

"All right, partner. Damn, this isn't going to help our cash flow. And we've got contracts to meet and no stock."

Sam looked grim. "We'll find a way around it. We always do. Some times are harder than others, is all."

"Travis, they're waiting." Mercy tugged his arm. With a final nod to Sam, he went.

Honey called him up beside her to thank him for his contribution to the night's effort. Her elfin features held an element of mischief as he tipped his hat in acknowledgment to the applauding crowd. Mercy went to the side of the stage where several large boxes sat waiting.

Honey continued. "And since everyone knows you're off to the National Finals in a couple of weeks, we'd like folks to have an opportunity to support the local champion with some proper equipment."

Travis gave the redhead a puzzled look. "Such as?"

"You'll see." She winked. "Now, everyone, we're going to ask you to bid on these items. Equipment goes to the champ, money into the task force fund, and remember, the higher the bid, the higher in our esteem we hold our local hero. So don't hurt his feelings—be generous. Ready, Travis?"

He didn't much like the feeling he was being set up, but shrugged gamely. "Fire away."

"Okay, Mercy." Honey waved. "Folks, what am I bid for the essential and totally unlovely designer neck brace?"

The crowd guffawed. Travis felt his ears begin to burn.

"Fifty cents," someone shouted.

"Oh, we can do better than that," Honey retorted. Mercy waved the foam rubber brace over her head, prancing back and forth like the round girl at a boxing match and earning wolf whistles.

"Twenty bucks," a young cowboy hollered.

Honey beamed. "Sold!"

Mercy sashayed to Travis and slipped the brace around his neck. Her eyes gleamed, and her voice was saccharine. "Here you go, cowboy. All yours. You're going to need it, I'll bet."

He didn't like her prediction, or being on display, but he fought back a surge of temper and gave the crowd a halfhearted smile. "Thanks."

But it wasn't over. In rapid order, Honey auctioned and Mercy adorned him in arm braces, slings, crutches, plastic casts and knee elastics until he was wrapped up like a mummy. He'd never felt so exposed, nor so foolish. The throng hooted at the final indignity—a wheelchair complete with oxygen tank. Mercy's antics as cover model raised the bidding time and again, adding nearly another thousand to the dollar total for the evening and sending Honey into raptures of gratitude as she wound up the auction.

"Thanks for being a good sport, Travis," she said. "Not that we expect you to come back to Flat Fork in this condition, but it pays to be prepared, right?"

"And thanks for that vote of confidence, Honey." All but hog-tied as he sat in the damned chair, mortified but trying to keep up a good face up, Travis forced a grin. He was quite certain he knew whose idea this little spectacle had been. If she wanted to play rough, he was more than willing.

"At least I've got my very own personal physician to give me a lot of tender loving care." He snatched Mercy's hand and tugged hard, pitching her across his lap. "Come here, darlin', and kiss my boo-boos all better."

He nuzzled her neck like a love-starved vampire. Sprawled over the wheelchair arms, skirts foaming, heels kicking, Mercy gasped and slapped at him, hissing under her breath. "Let me go, you lousy polecat."

The crowd loved it. Hoots and catcalls filled the hall as Mercy scrambled to her feet with her cheeks on fire. Honey was laughing so hard she could barely speak.

"Any sacrifice for a good cause, right, cowboy? Let's give this couple another hand for all their help and get this party started again."

To enthusiastic applause, Travis waved as Mercy shoved the wheelchair offstage with a force that rattled his teeth. The band cranked up again. Travis tugged at the knots on an arm sling and tried to get up. "Give me a hand with this rigging, darlin'?"

"You can stay tied up till doomsday for all I care."

He grinned. "You mean you didn't like the way your little lesson for me turned out?" He knew he'd hit the mark when her face grew even redder. "If you can't stand the heat, stay out of the kitchen. Besides, with my brand on you, those greasy-handed galoots will keep their distance now."

"Your brand—?" Fury made her eyes blaze blue fire. "I'm no man's property—least of all yours."

She stepped off the bandstand and stormed toward the exit.

"Mercy, wait."

"Go to hell."

Stifling a curse, Travis wrenched off braces and bandages and struggled to his feet, only to have Honey rush up just then to gush out her thanks. The next time he looked up, Mercy had vanished.

Six

"**G**et in the truck." Shoving open the passenger door, Travis let his vehicle pace beside Mercy, who was marching down the cold, dark sidewalk on the quiet outskirts of town. The crisp wind whipped her hair around her face. Head up, jaw tight, she didn't pause, didn't even look his way.

"No, thank you."

He cursed violently. "I've been looking for you over an hour. Come on, get inside."

"No."

He lost it then. Slamming on his brakes, he vaulted from the driver's side, charging around the hood of the ebony truck. She turned, her eyes gleaming in the dim glow of the street lamp, fending him off with a raised hand.

"Get away from me, Travis. I'm warning you—"

He grabbed her upper arms through her coat, spinning

her around against the fender so that she gave a startled yelp. "I've had just about all I can take, do you understand me?"

Her chin shot up, and her mouth tightened. Her palms pressed against his shearling jacket. "And I don't suffer fools gladly, cowboy."

"Even a fool can be right sometimes," he muttered darkly.

"Let go, damn you."

He showed his teeth. "This is Texas, remember? There's a law that says 'leave with the one who brought you.'"

"So sue me."

"By God, I brought you, I'll see you home." His eyes narrowed, and he grabbed her waist, jerking her against him. "Unless there's something else you'd rather do, something we've been putting off too long...."

"I'd sooner bunk with a rattlesnake."

"Yeah, well, you aren't so sweet yourself sometimes, but that hasn't for one second changed the fact we're so hot for each other we're about to go up in flames." At her outraged gasp, he tugged her even closer, the flat of his palm rubbing over her middle in a seductive sweep, tugging at her shirt hem, touching the sizable metal buckle at her waistband. Then he stiffened, went absolutely still, really seeing it for the first time. "What the hell is this?"

She didn't answer, merely looked down her patrician nose at him in silent challenge. But he recognized the buckle, one of the first championship ones Kenny had won. And she'd chosen to wear it tonight, like some kind of symbolic chastity belt, a barrier between the past and the present that said it all.

Anger warred with despair. He want to choke her. He wanted to howl like a lone wolf. Because he loved this woman, always had, always would, and there was nothing within his power he could do to reach her, not when she was determined to resist him even to this extent. Not when it was clear she wouldn't, couldn't forgive him for what he'd done all those many years ago.

Slowly he uncurled his fingers and took a step back. She watched him warily, as if sensing he stood on the edge of violence. Her look cut him to his very soul, and he knew he was beaten.

"All right, darlin', you win." His words rasped in his throat like broken glass. "Just let me take you home, and we'll call it quits, that's all I ask."

Mercy didn't protest when he drew her around to the open passenger door and helped her inside the truck. As he drove, she watched him with big eyes from her corner, her mouth drooping, the battle over, but the cost in life and energy dear indeed.

Travis drove automatically, his mind tossed in a maelstrom of broken dreams and shattered hopes. There didn't seem to be anything to say. And then suddenly he knew there was, some things past due that he'd been too afraid to risk for fear of driving her even further away. But now, when all that was left was a final goodbye, he knew he couldn't end it without putting at least this much right.

A road he recognized intersected the main highway, and he turned onto the bumpy, gravel track.

"This isn't the way home," she said.

"No. I've got something to say. It won't take long."

He drew the truck to a halt on a little bare knoll under a stand of water oaks overlooking a trickle of a creek and killed the engine. O'Neal Lane was a place used by generations of sparking teenagers. Travis had spent many an hour wooing the local cowgirls out here, every one except the one gal who sat so still and quiet beside him now. He stared out the dark windshield, bouncing his fists lightly against the steering wheel, wondering where to start. He sighed. He guessed at the beginning.

"We never talked about the night Kenny died."

She stiffened. "You weren't around."

"I was pretty messed up after it happened. I made a lot of mistakes."

"Don't do this." There was an undeniable note of pleading in her voice.

Removing his hat, he set it on the dash, rubbed his palms down his face and shook his head. "We've left it too long, Mercy. I know you can't ever forgive me, and I guess I have to understand that no matter what I want from you, it'll always be between us."

"What are you talking about?"

"I was driving. It was raining, and that other truck came out of nowhere, but I'd had one too many beers. It was my fault. Kenny was my best friend, and I loved him like a brother, but I took him from you. If it hadn't been for me...I just want you to know I'm sorry. I never said it, and I know it doesn't change anything, but I wanted you to know."

Throat tight, he groped for the ignition key.

"All this time...oh, God." Blindly, she reached out, her fingers trembling on his arm.

He froze. "Mercy?"

"I never blamed you." Her voice was raw and anguished in the darkness. "It wasn't you. *I* killed him."

Mercy sensed his shock, his horror, and the guilt of fifteen years threatened to overwhelm her. She buried her face in her cold hands, her shoulders shaking.

"You're going to have to explain that," Travis said carefully.

"You weren't supposed to be on that road."

"I don't understand."

Raising her head, she let her hands fall lifelessly into her lap, and her voice was dull with regret. "He'd had a big win that night. You were celebrating, planning on staying over, he said when he called. But then something changed, and he insisted on making that long haul home. Do you remember?"

Travis nodded slowly. "Yeah. I was ticked off for about the first hundred miles or so, but he was in a god-awful hurry to get back to Flat Fork all of a sudden."

"And you never wondered why?"

"I figured he just wanted to get home to you."

Her laugh was tinny, painful. "Right. To the girl who'd just broken up with him. Long distance, no less."

Travis jerked. "What?"

"If I'd only had the courage to wait to face him, neither of you would have been on the highway that night. I was the one who made it happen, don't you see?" She choked. "I was the one who told him over the phone I didn't want to see him, that I didn't love him."

"You broke it off. But why? You were crazy about each other...."

She couldn't answer for the lump of emotion clotting her throat, her gaze stark with shame and self-recrimination as she looked at him. She saw comprehension dawn in Travis's expression.

"God."

At his whispered word, an intolerable wave of guilt crashed over her, and she fled, opening the truck door and stumbling out. He caught up with her within a few steps, grasping her shoulders from behind and pulling her struggling form back against his chest. The pale yellow light from the inside cab fixture made her feel exposed and vulnerable, and she turned her head aside, praying for the darkness to conceal her sin, knowing that it couldn't any longer.

"Mercy, darlin'—"

"How can you bear to call me that?" she cried, torn to her soul with anguish. "I did it to you, too. All this time, blaming yourself for the accident, when it was me— the selfish, spoiled brat—who decided to hurt a decent young man for no better reason than that she had the hots for his best friend."

Travis turned her in his arms, his voice rough. "Don't do this to yourself. We were young. These things happen."

"Excuses. I knew better. But I got what I deserved. Kenny gone, and then you, too. I lost you both."

"I couldn't face you. After what I'd done, I was afraid of what I'd see."

"Afraid? Of what?"

"Your hatred."

Her eyes widened. "No. Never that."

"But I didn't know it, couldn't risk it. You weren't the only one feeling guilty."

"I know. The accident—"

He gripped her arms tighter, shaking his head. "No, not just that. God Almighty, Mercy! I was head-over-heels in love with you. How could you not have seen that?"

Mercy quivered, her breath leaving her lungs in a little puff. "I—I—"

"Surprised?" His mouth twisted with a curl of self-mockery. "Maybe I was a better actor back then than I thought. I sure as hell knew I was a sorry bastard for wanting to betray my best friend every time I looked at you."

She licked her lips. "We both sensed it."

"Yes. And fought it."

"Not hard enough."

"We'd have figured something out eventually. If things had only worked out differently...."

"Yes, if only..."

"At least we know the truth now." He shook his head, and his fingers flexed on her arms. "God help us, Mercy. The denial, the guilt—we've been trapped and didn't even realize it. And neither of us can take the blame any longer. You've got to promise me that much. We've both got to let this—him—go."

Looking up at Travis, she felt a tear slide from the corner of her eye. "We've wasted so much time."

"You're the doc," he said gently. "Some wounds just take longer to heal."

She gave a watery snort. "Coming from you, cowboy, that's almost funny."

"Oh, hell. Just come here."

She went willingly, sliding into his arms, seeking his warmth as a sob broke from her depths, the sound ratcheting up in a release of denial and pain fifteen years overdue. Pulling her close, he leaned back against the truck's open doorframe, bracing himself so that she half lay against his chest. She clung to him, her arms around his trim waist underneath his jacket, her cheek pressed to the dark cotton of the shirt she drenched with her tears. His fingers threaded through her hair, and his lips brushed her forehead.

"You just go ahead and bawl, darlin'," he said, his own voice thick. "I reckon it's been a long time coming."

She raised her head, reaching for him, her fingers framing his lean cheeks, not surprised to find them as damp as her own. "For both of us, Travis."

Their eyes met. Mercy stroked his stubbled jaw. He

thumbed the tender place on the nape of her neck. He bent his head. She stretched upward. Mouths melded softly. Sighs whispered in benediction, forgiveness, comfort.

He felt like home. As familiar as a favorite chair. As welcoming as a crackling fireplace on a cold winter's eve. As loving as a mother's touch.

Sweet sensation warmed her. The velvety brush of his mustache against her skin. The rasp of his callused fingertips stroking her neck. The supple curve of his lips sipping hers, no demands, only tenderness.

She flowed against him, her breasts flattened by the hard wall of his chest. Touching his face, his hair, she poured all the charity and sweetness that was in her into the kiss, willing him to feel her gratitude and affection for a friend regained, something lost and now restored in its most precious form.

Travis broke the kiss reluctantly, pressing his forehead against hers. "Aw, sweet Mercy..."

Her voice was an ache. "I've missed you so much."

"There wasn't a day I didn't think about you."

"I'm glad we can be friends again."

"Pals."

She smiled and ran her forefinger over his mustache. *"Compadres."*

"Amigos." He caught her wrist and nuzzled her fingertips, his breath warm on her skin.

Shivering, but not with the chill in the night air, she gazed at the wonderfully masculine line of his mouth, then looked up into his dark eyes. A moment of hesitation, then they moved as one, his mouth claiming hers as eagerly as hers did his, lips slanting, clinging, in an electrifying exchange of heat.

She couldn't breathe. He parted her lips with his tongue

and took total possession of her senses. She retaliated, nipping at him, giving back as much as she got, digging her fingers into the thick hair at his nape in an effort to stay on her feet. His hands were inside her coat, cupping her breasts. Groaning, she pressed closer, shrugging out of the garment, sliding her knee between his thighs.

They broke apart, gasping, both quailed and exalted by the unexpected explosion of need. Everything spun inside Mercy's head—the old forbidden excitement, their new-found sweetness, this insistent chemistry that could not be denied. Confusion, longing, curiosity—she was dizzy with it all. And the reckless Mercy knew exactly what she wanted.

"Do that again," she said.

The skin of his jaw stretched taut, and his voice was gravelly. "You've got to be careful what you ask of a man as hungry as I am."

"I'm hungry, too."

Faster than the blink of an eye, he turned and pressed her shoulders against the side of the truck cab, making her gasp with surprise, catching that gasp with a fiery kiss that melted her knees into jelly. When he'd taken every molecule of air from her overheated lungs, he lifted his head, trailing hot kisses down her neck while he opened her shirt. The chilly night air whispered over her wisp of a bra, puckering her nipples against the lacy fabric. Overwhelmed and exhilarated, knowing he was as out of control as she felt, Mercy smiled as he slipped out of his jacket. Reaching up, she ripped open the pearl snaps on his Western shirt, exposing the marvel of his muscular chest.

When she ran her palms across his nipples, he groaned and tugged at her shirttail, pulling it from the waistband of her skirt, then hesitated as his fingers brushed the cool metal buckle. He drew back, but she met his eyes unwaveringly. Never breaking the intensity of their locked gazes, she unbuckled the belt, then threw it toward the blackness of the distant creekbed with all her might.

It was enough.

With a growl of approval, Travis scooped her close, lifted her, then took a step to the open passenger door and pressed her down onto the length of truck seat. He followed her down, half-in and half-out of the vehicle, his mouth on her breasts, laving the crested peaks through the lace of her bra, until she writhed and moaned with incoherent pleasure.

"We're liable to get arrested," she said, holding his head to steady him on her flesh.

"No one around for miles, darlin'." Impatient with the fabric barrier, he found the clasp, released it and bared her breasts fully. He brushed his mustache over the creamy mounds, then lightly licked one budded tip.

She arched, said in a strangled voice, "The light—"

He slapped at the cab light, killed it, fumbled the radio on, filled the air with a late-night country station. She clawed open his shirt cuffs, pushed the garment from his shoulders in a frenzy that had him shrugging to help her.

"I used to dream about being out here with you."

"You brought all the girls here to make out. They used to talk about what a stud you were."

"It was never the right girl. Until now. Touch me, darlin'."

She obliged, sliding her hands across his broad shoulders, down his sides, into the dip of his jeans. He caught her mouth again, drugging kisses that swamped her synapses, melted her down to her core. She pressed her palm against the hard outline of his manhood and was rewarded with a groan.

Travis found the hem of her flounced skirt, shoved the foamy material aside and ran his hands over her kneecaps, up the satiny length of her thighs to the silk-covered juncture at the top. He probed her mysteries through the thin fabric, groaning against her lips as she lurched against him.

"You're so wet, so hot..." Breath gusting, he laid his cheek against her breast, shuddering. "Sorry."

"Sorry—?"

"I never meant a little making out to go this far."

She could feel his withdrawal, and everything in her rejected it. "No!" She clasped him to her, whispered fiercely, "I...we need this."

"Yes."

Reaching down, she found the fastener on his jeans, released it, freeing his surging sex and stroking him intimately. He went wild, tossing her skirts, sliding her panties down her legs, pushing off her boots. Catching her beneath her hips, he positioned her on the edge of the seat, then probed her petals with his tip, sliding into her silkiness with a care that maddened Mercy. Rising to meet him, she clasped her arms around his neck, found his mouth with hers, then locked her legs around his hips and, with a wordless demand as old as time, forced him to give her everything.

It was exquisite. She'd never experienced such fullness, such fiery heat, such a sense of rightness and completion. She'd been waiting an eternity for this, for him, and she hadn't even realized it. Tears of joy filled her eyes. Then he began to move, and thought became impossible.

His hands moved on her breasts, teasing cords of sensation that unfurled and lodged low. Mouth rapacious and demanding, he mimicked the rhythms of their bodies with his tongue, stealing what remained of her breath. Thrusting slowly, until she screamed inwardly with frustration. Building the tempo, smoothly, powerfully filling her over and over until she was blind and mindless, a slave to the sensation of him deep within her being, to the knowledge that they were one entity, exploring a universe of possibilities together.

And then the impossible happened, and her body clenched around him, splintering her with an explosion of pleasure so powerful she felt the world dim. On and on, and there was only Travis, who made her world bright again, a sunrise shared as he cried out her name and found his own fulfillment.

Afterward, with her cheeks wet, he held her close against himself. Locked together in the cramped space, they were both dazed, both wondering. And over the radio Judy Collins crooned about a damned ole rodeo....

Seven

It was obvious he'd been whopped upside the head once too often. Or else he'd simply been born a damned idiot.

Travis climbed out of his truck into the bright morning sunshine, then strode through the double glass doors straight into the melee that was the usual order of business at Doc Hazelton's Flat Fork Hospital Clinic.

Clerks behind a glassed-in counter waved manila files. Red-faced babies screeched in their mothers' arms. Elderly men in overalls waited stoically, their blue-haired wives sitting beside them on the hard plastic chairs crocheting or flipping through five-year-old magazines. Nurses in pink scrubs appeared at the examination room doors and called names. A hulking teenage boy wearing a Flat Fork High football jersey and a knee brace arranged his crutches and looked bored.

Travis hesitated, scanning the throng, then felt a familiar gut punch when he spotted Mercy's blond head bent over the morning newspaper. Lord, he loved her. The sight of her never failed to stir him. And after what they'd shared the night before...

He grimaced, cussing himself. No class at all, King. None.

Making love to her on the front seat of his damn truck. Steaming up the windows. Getting it on like a pair of horny teenagers. Forget that it was the best damn thing that had ever happened to him. Forget that he'd figured he could go to his Maker at that moment, at peace at last because he'd found Mercy again after all those lonely years and made her his.

But the lady deserved better than a quick toss in the hay with a rambunctious cowpoke. She needed candlelight and wooing, sweet nothings and slow hands. They needed time together to learn each other all over again, to find out that being lovers was even better than being friends. And maybe when that became clear to her, then he could say words like *forever* and *always* and she'd believe he meant it.

Unfortunately, as usual for a man who spent most of his life on the road, time was at a premium.

"You're one hard lady to track down, darlin'."

She looked up with a small start of surprise, her cheeks going rosy. She wore jeans and a soft fuzzy sweater that showed off her breasts, and her hair was in a knot that his fingers itched to take down. "Travis. What are you doing here?"

"Looking for you. Your mother said you'd brought the judge in for his thousand-mile checkup."

Her lips twitched. "My mother never said anything of the sort. Too undignified."

"Words to that effect, then." He took her hand. "Talk to me?"

Her eyes flicked to the door leading to the examining rooms. "Daddy's liable to be through with Doc any minute."

"I won't take longer than that."

He drew her to her feet, looked around, then towed her through another set of doors that led into the deserted main lobby of the hospital. The area was populated only by the lone telephone operator behind a high counter and a row of cold drink machines against the far wall. Travis pushed Mercy into the corner out of eyeshot behind one of the machines, bent his head and kissed her.

She tasted of toothpaste and morning coffee and something inexplicably female and unique only to her. Leaning her against the wall, he braced both palms flat beside her head and feasted. Caught off guard, she stiffened momentarily, then resistance melted away, her soft lips clinging to his, a little murmur in her throat that made his pulse pound.

He drew back, pleased at her dazed expression, groaning at the blood pooling in his loins. He'd been loath to leave her last night, would have stayed camped out in the cold truck until dawn if he'd had his druthers, but common sense and a strange and shy reticence in the aftermath of their passion had made him see reason and return her, however reluctantly, to the Holt mansion. To his way of thinking, leaving her on her doorstep had been a highly unsatisfying ending to an emotional evening, and he was going to do his best to make certain that wasn't a lasting impression.

"Good morning," he said into her ear.

She caught a shuddering breath, tried to focus, then seemed to realize their exposed position. "You—someone will see."

"We're alone. Well, almost. And no one's watching,

anyway. So I may as well—'' He wrung another kiss from her, and his own breathing was even gustier when he released her again. "God, it seems like a thousand years have passed since last night."

Pink stained her cheeks, and her lashes fanned down in embarrassment. "Travis, please."

"I had to see you before I left."

She looked up, her bluebonnet eyes wide and startled. "You're going? Where?"

"Albuquerque." He grinned. "Everything all packed up and ready to go out in the truck. Couple of bulls with my name on 'em waiting for me."

She slumped against the wall. "Oh."

"Just for the weekend." He tugged a lock of hair free at her nape and curled it around his finger. "I'll be back before you know it."

"I see."

The forced neutrality of her tone disturbed him. He put a knuckle under her chin, obliging her to look at him. "I know a lot happened fast, darlin'. And maybe not the way we expected. Hell, a pickup truck wasn't what I'd imagined, either. I wanted it to be first class for you all the way down the line, champagne and satin sheets. I promise, I'll make it up to you."

"No, that's all right. I—"

Inspiration hit him, and he snapped his fingers. "In fact, there's no reason not to make a start on it. Come with me."

She inhaled sharply. "What?"

"To Albuquerque. We'll do the town after the rodeo." He bobbled his eyebrows in a licentious leer. "And I guarantee there'll be a real bed in the picture, room service, the works. What do you say?"

She swallowed hard and shook her head. "I can't. Daddy—"

"Is on the mend. Surely he can spare you a couple of days?"

"No, really, I couldn't."

"But—"

"It's not a good idea." Her words were unexpectedly sharp.

His eyes narrowed. Hands curled into fists, her back against the wall, she watched him warily. Alarms went off inside his brain. "Okay, what's really going on?"

"Nothing. It just isn't wise to rush into something."

"Rush? I don't call fifteen years being in a hurry."

She bit her lip. "But nothing's really changed."

Dumbfounded, he mouthed a curse. "The hell it hasn't. Look me in the eye and tell me what happened last night didn't mean anything."

"It—it can't." She swallowed, and her gaze skittered away from his. "We got carried away by old memories, that's all. But we're not kids anymore, and nostalgia isn't enough. You have your life, and I have mine. They'll never mesh, don't you see? I can't even bear the idea of seeing you ride those damned bulls. To try to pretend we can put it together is just going to hurt us both. We have to stop this before that happens."

A giant hand squeezed his chest. Pain and burgeoning anger thickened his voice. "The hell you say."

"Travis, be reasonable. It was the heat of the moment, and a mistake for both of us that we can't repeat. It's the only thing that makes sense."

That she would try to intellectualize the passion they'd shared in such a cool fashion drove him berserk. He caught her shoulders, jerked her against himself. "Make sense out of *this*."

He ground his lips against hers, infuriated, intent on staking a claim she couldn't deny. She held herself stiffly, not fighting him, but rigidly withholding the response he knew lay within her. He released her with a low growl of frustration.

Her eyes were icy. "Satisfied?"

"Not by a long shot. You're running away again, and that never solves anything."

"I'm making a decision that's right for me." She drew herself up with a frigid dignity. "I hope you'll accept it gracefully."

"Hope away, darlin'." Travis jabbed a finger in her face. "I'm mad enough to eat the Devil with his horns on, so don't think for one minute this is over. We've got something special, and there's no fighting it, if you're smart."

"I suppose that's a matter of opinion, so we'll see, won't we?"

"Hell, I don't have time to stand around jawing about last night just because you're so scared you'd rather tuck tail and run than admit you never had it so good."

She hissed in a breath of pure outrage. "Don't flatter yourself, cowboy."

He laughed, a hard sound. "You just think about how it was until I get back. I'll bet you stay wet."

"You low-down coyote." Fury made her eyes burn. "Go to hell, or to Albuquerque—it's all the same—and ride your stupid bulls, but stay away from me!"

Travis stepped back, his mouth twisting. "Yeah, maybe you'll get lucky and I'll break my damn neck this go round. That would solve all your problems, wouldn't it, darlin'?"

She paled as though he'd slapped her, but he didn't have it in him at the moment to feel any remorse. She was doing her best to throw it all away, and for what? Well, damn her pride, damn her fear, damn her!

With a mocking tip of his hat brim, he stormed through the glass entrance doors, Albuquerque bound. His last glimpse of her through the wavy distortion of the windows was of her white face, and her father appearing at her side, staring through the panes after Travis, his judge's countenance creased with condemnation.

A Blue Norther roiled on the horizon late Sunday afternoon, sullen navy clouds splatting occasional leaden raindrops in the path of the advancing front, the whole county poised and apprehensive, awaiting the storm's arrival with its potential for violence and destruction. Hands clenched on the steering wheel, Mercy scowled at the scudding clouds and eased her convertible over the metal cattle gap leading into the Prestons' Lazy Diamond Ranch.

The weather did nothing to assuage the tension that had been building in her bones since her last confrontation with Travis. It was all she could do to keep her mounting fear from completely paralyzing her. *Break my damn neck...*

Irrational as she knew it to be, she felt as though she'd spoken a dire curse over him, and the premonition of disaster that had been swelling within her had reached the point of explosion, driving her from the Holt mansion in search of some relief.

Mercy rubbed her damp palms against her heather knit pants and reached to turn the heater down. She was sweating under her coat at the thought that it was just like Kenny all over again, the nightmare revisited, her rejection the catalyst that brought calamity down on all their heads. Travis had been wild and angry, as only a man whose pride had been pricked could be, and that meant he'd be careless.

Lord, she'd never forgive herself if something happened to him. She couldn't stand the suspense of not knowing any longer and so found herself on this road, heading for the only people who'd know for sure. She didn't even care if she made a fool of herself.

Bumping over the gravel track leading to the ranch house, Mercy grimaced. *Fool* didn't even begin to describe her. She must have been insane to want Travis so badly that she'd forgotten all her usual caution. It had been the old, reckless, selfish Mercy who'd made love like a wanton on the front seat of a pickup and damned the consequences. What a fool. What a mistake.

It was glorious, her memory whispered. Wonderful and magical beyond all imagining.

But wrong, she told herself sternly. Wrong because he was still a man whose life was on the line almost daily. He was right to call her a coward. She'd lost to death before, and she didn't want to face that kind of heartache ever again. She couldn't give her heart to Travis, only to have him maimed or killed before her eyes. That didn't make her craven exactly, just a sensible woman. Hadn't she suffered enough? Did she have to lose everyone she cared about? And of course she cared about the hardheaded cowboy. He was her friend, after all, no matter what.

But it was safer to guard her feelings. He was who he was, and while she was grateful they'd finally cleared the air after all these years, she just wasn't going to risk it. He'd have to understand. She only wished she did herself.

Mercy parked the car in front of the neat, white ranch house and climbed out, holding her hair against the snapping wind, squinting against the cold sting of raindrops.

The front door swung inward, and Roni Preston stood on the threshold, holding the screen door open with a distressed expression on her face and gesturing for Mercy to hurry.

Mercy's heart lurched uncontrollably. Scrambling through the needle-sharp bombardment, she vaulted up the slick steps, quaking in every fiber. "What is it? It's Travis, isn't it? Tell me."

Roni's dark eyes were puzzled. "Travis? What about him?"

"He's been hurt, hasn't he?" She didn't recognize the shrill voice as her own.

"No, he's fine." Roni touched her shoulder, frowning. "Heard from him just an hour ago. Drew a bull called Black Sabbath and rode that sucker straight into the first place winner's money."

"Thank God." Light-headed with relief, Mercy licked her damp lips and swallowed hard. "You looked so...so...I thought—"

"Lord, you are in a state, aren't you?" Throwing an arm around Mercy's shoulders, Roni drew her inside toward the cozy kitchen, pushed her down on a trestle bench at the table and took her coat. "Sit down before you fall down, and I'll make us a cup of tea. Sam's out seeing to the stock, and I'm frazzled out of my gourd because Jessie's teething." From the rear of the house came a child's fractious wail. "There she goes again."

"Then I shouldn't disturb you."

Roni waved Mercy back to her seat and cocked her head to one side. After a few snuffles, silence prevailed. Roni smiled and reached for the teakettle. "Good, she needs to finish her nap, and I could use some adult conversation. I'm glad you came by. Anxious about Travis, were you?"

"Uh…I'd just had a bad feeling all day." The uncertainty still churned in her stomach, but she shrugged and tried to smile. "Silly, I guess."

"For worrying that two-thousand pounds of snot-slinging tornado might stomp on him? I don't think that's so silly." Roni set two cups of steaming herbal tea and a plate of sugar cookies shaped like turkeys and cornucopias on the table and joined Mercy. "I've thought for a while he can't keep it up much longer."

"He thinks he can."

"Well, I suppose pulling down the top prize money proves he's right. And Lord knows, with this rash of rustling, King and Preston Stock Company can use the cash flow."

Mercy curled her cold fingers around the mug and took a sip of tea. She didn't want to care about Travis's problems, but she did. "It's that bad?"

"Bad enough. The business isn't that old, and Buzz Henry's still so ticked Sam and Travis joined forces to compete against him, he's liable to do anything to eat our lunch. This pinch we're in sure does hit a man right where he lives—in his dadgum pride. Sam's been as ornery as a bear with a sore paw."

Mercy could certainly relate to that, and she chuckled at the other woman's put-out expression. "It's got to be something in the DNA."

"You said it. They can't believe someone actually has the audacity to steal from us, much less that they can't figure out who it is."

"The police aren't having any luck, either, I take it?"

Roni bit the tail feathers off a sugar cookie turkey and shook her curls. "Not a bit. The sheriff says it could be kids, and Honey is keeping her eyes peeled."

"What about that boy at the ball game—Chase?"

"Honey talked to his uncle. Dan Conly's a reclusive galoot who's been on the wrong side of the law a time or two himself, but he insists the kid's clean. Now, I'm not so sure about Chase's companions, but none of the local packing houses or auction barns have had any suspicious activity, and our cattle are being hauled off slick as a whistle, so it must be a professional operation."

"The sheriff will solve it eventually, I'm sure."

"Well, Sam's not taking any more chances with Grenada. He's sure that prime bull's going to be our bread and butter for quite a while, so he's going to move him to Travis's place for safekeeping."

"I certainly hope you don't have any more trouble." Mercy took a final swig from the mug and set it aside. "I should get back. Daddy gets as cranky as your little Jessie this time of the day, and I like to give Mother a break."

They rose and went to the door. Roni's gaze was both teasing and speculative. "So, should I tell Travis you drove all the way out here just to check up on his health?"

Mercy grimaced and shrugged into her coat. "I'm sure he's got lots of ladies looking out for him, so don't feed his ego on my account."

"Well, he's always had a reputation as quite a womanizer—not that I noticed any of the womenfolk complaining—but lately I'd say that his attentions have been rather, er—focused."

Mercy sighed. "He's never been one to resist a challenge, either, but that's all I represent, believe me."

"I'm not so sure. The way he looks at you..."

"It's the chase that interests Travis King," she said lightly. "He wouldn't know what to do if he caught me, and I've got better sense than to get involved with a man with a death wish. Anyway, the cowboy's a tumbleweed.

He'll forget all about this latest hunt when I go back to Ft. Worth.''

"When's that?"

Mercy longed to say today, tomorrow, before Travis got home. She dreaded another confrontation with him, knowing nothing would be changed, but to hightail it back to the city would be tantamount to admitting he was right about her running away. No, she'd just have to stick it out a few more days.

"I'm planning on leaving the day after Thanksgiving," she told Roni. "Daddy's coming along well, and I've got to get back to work." She wondered why the prospect held so little appeal.

Roni looked disappointed. "It's been nice having you home. You'll come to the all-county Thanksgiving service Wednesday evening, won't you?"

"Mother mentioned something about it."

"I'm singing in the choir, believe it or not, so be warned."

Mercy laughed. "Well, in that case, I wouldn't miss it for the world."

"I'll see you there. And, Mercy?"

"Yes?" She paused halfway across the porch.

"Travis is just about the most decent fellow I know, next to Sam." Roni's warm brown eyes were full of understanding. "Don't sell him short. Or yourself, either."

It was a hell of a note, Travis thought sourly, to roll into town after a two-day drive with a fat winner's check in your back pocket, all set to be the conquering hero, and the only thing you could do to celebrate was hit the drugstore for painkillers and put your aching body to bed. Alone.

Travis climbed carefully out of his truck in front of

Kelly's Pharmacy Monday afternoon. The blustery day was damp and cold as a witch's caress, and he shivered under his shearling jacket and gritted his teeth at the sizzling jolt of pain that started in the small of his back and raced down his leg. He hadn't even taken that much of a pounding in Albuquerque. Mercy would no doubt point out that a lifetime of abuse was bound to catch up with him sooner or later. He'd rather wrestle a turpentined bobcat than give her the satisfaction, though.

It was enough to put a man off his feed. Or make him think about options. And he would, just as soon as he stopped hurting.

He entered the modest pharmacy, dim and warm from the old-fashioned gas heaters positioned at ceiling level in the back corners of the cluttered store. Plucking an assortment of over-the-counter painkillers from the shelves, he made his way to the rear, then came up short at the sight of a group of teenage boys crowding the checkout counter. It was the same gang he'd seen at the football game, including the little dark-haired twerp who lived out his way, Chase Conly. No matter what Honey said, he didn't think he could trust the kid as far as he could throw him.

Missy Armitage, the pretty, blond clerk, blew her fair curls out of her eyes and pursed her mouth in exasperation. "Are you rowdies *sure* this is all this time?"

A pug-faced eighteen-year-old in a plaid CPO jacket tossed an opened bag of potato chips on the counter beside the register. "Ain't paying for these. They're rancid."

"They can't have been. You ate them," Missy protested.

"Thought the customer was always right, Missy, honey." The teenager leered and caressed the girl's shoulder.

She yanked away. "Lay off, Clayton. You're such a jerk."

"These jokers giving you a hard time, darlin'?" Travis asked, his tone easy and his eyes hard.

He walked through the group and set his bottles on the counter. A couple of the boys shuffled their feet. Chase recognized his neighbor with an uneasy glance. Clayton straightened into a belligerent pose that all but said "try to knock this chip off my shoulder."

"Why don't you cow patties pay the lady and vamoose?" Travis suggested. "She's got other customers waiting."

"Our money's as good as yours," Clayton growled.

"So use it, partner. Before I lose what's left of my good humor."

Clayton met him eye-to-eye, decided he didn't like what he saw, then muttered and tossed some bills on the counter. Gratefully, Missy rang up his purchases.

Travis glanced at Chase. He was a wiry thirteen, underdressed for the weather in jeans and worn sweatshirt, dark-eyed and so uncertain about becoming a man he had to keep himself puffed up with piss and vinegar all the time. Travis remembered the feeling. "You cutting school today, Chase?"

A dull red stole over the boy's freckled cheekbones. He glanced at his companions, then drew himself up with a sneer. "You live on Mars, mister? It's vacation week."

"And none of you can find anything better to do than harass a lady? So much for the Code of the West." Travis narrowed his gaze. "You been hanging out around my place again?"

Chase stiffened. "No, why?"

"Some of my stock's come up missing. Maybe you varmints saw something?"

"Naw, we ain't seen nuthin'." Clayton scooped his change into his pocket and shoved Chase toward the front. The other boys meandered with assumed casualness after them. "Let's go. Got better things to do than stand around jawing with crippled-up has-been cowboys."

Travis hooked a thumb into his belt loop and watched them leave. The kid was closer to the truth than he wanted to admit, but that didn't mean he had to like it.

"Thanks, Travis," Missy said. "That bunch really gets on my nerves, always trying to impress folks with how tough they are."

"Yeah, it's a pretty good act if you can get away with it."

"Will this be all?" She pointed at the painkillers.

He was tempted to say yes, but the throbbing in his lower back told him not to play the fool. "Better get me a refill on that prescription Doc Hazelton gave me last time, too."

She smiled cheerfully. "Sure thing. Be just a jiff."

While he waited, Travis rubbed his mustache and thought about Chase Conly. There was a tension in the boy that boded ill and a willingness to play the tough guy for his older buddies that was sure to get him in a pile of trouble—if it hadn't already. And he could swear the boy knew something about the missing stock. Maybe he ought to give Honey Jones a call.

"Here you go, Travis." Missy held out a small sack. "I charged it to you."

"Thanks. See you around." He tipped his hat and tried not to make his hobbling walk too noticeable. He was just stiff, he decided, and a couple of doses of medicine and some ice packs would make him good as new. And he certainly needed to be up to fighting form, because he still had a stubborn woman to deal with.

Yes, sir, he and Mercy were going to have it out. Just as soon as he stopped hurting.

Eight

"Good Lord, girl! What the devil have you been up to so early?"

Holding a bone china coffee cup and wearing a cashmere cardigan, Jonathan watched his daughter from the doorway of his study, his expression startled.

"Tractor accident." In mud- and blood-splattered slacks and sweater, Mercy paused at the base of the stairs. Her dirty sneakers smeared the polished marble tiles, and she knew she risked Daisy's wrath for sullying the foyer's pristine appearance the day before the Thanksgiving holiday. "I rode in the ambulance for Doc."

"You seem to have gotten the worst of it."

Shoving a hand through her loose hair, she shook her head. "Believe me, no. Ben Honicutt did, but I think he's going to be all right."

"I'm glad to hear it." Jonathan lifted a tufted eyebrow. "You've been busy as a beaver with a load of new twigs for three solid days, but could you spare us a minute? I've got coffee."

Glancing at her watch, she followed him into the study. "Doc's got me scheduled for another house call—"

She broke off at the sight of the trio of visitors seated in a semicircle around the judge's big mahogany desk: Honey Jones, a bit pale behind her glasses, her elfin features creased with anxiety, and Sam Preston and Travis in Western shirts and vests, both rising to their feet at Mercy's entrance, nodding and mouthing greetings.

"Morning, Mercy. Roni enjoyed your visit."

"Hello, darlin'."

Mercy gulped, speared by Travis's accusing regard, chilled by the ominous tone in his gravel-rough voice. She'd never dreamed that brown eyes could be so cold and frustrated and so hot and hungry at the same time. Guilt and fear and lust washed through her like a storm tide.

She was too busy to face this, she thought frantically. She had a thousand errands to accomplish for her mother before she returned to Ft. Worth. And then she'd been pitching in like a demon to help poor overextended Doc Hazelton. Could she help it if her schedule over the last couple of days had been running at her usual hectic pace? It was unfortunate, but she'd just not had the time or opportunity to return Travis's phone calls. Daisy reported he'd even come by the day before, looking for her, but of course she hadn't been home. She wasn't making herself scarce out of spite. It was just the nature of things for busy people.

Yeah, right, you coward. Lie to everyone else, but don't lie to yourself.

The truth was she was running, spinning as fast as a hamster in an exercise wheel, doing anything, everything, to avoid another confrontation with Travis that would serve no useful purpose and change nothing. She knew it. He knew it. And her strategy had been working just fine. Until now.

"I—I'm sorry," Mercy stammered, taking a step back. "I didn't realize you had visitors. I won't disturb you—"

"Nonsense," Jonathan replied, taking her elbow and firmly ushering her toward an empty straight chair between Travis and Honey. "This is a task force powwow. You know King and Preston stock's being rustled, don't you?"

"Yes, I heard, but—"

"So Travis spots a gang of teenage boys hanging around his place, and Honey's been having a time with them—"

"Well, some of them, anyway," the juvenile officer interjected. "Not that I couldn't handle a few misdemeanor, truancy, and pure-dee boy-mischief complaints. But now I get worrisome reports that Clayton and a couple of his buddies are throwing money around like they have it to burn. These boys usually don't have two plug nickels to rub together."

Mercy flicked a glance at Travis, then back to the judge. "You've got proof they're behind the thefts?"

Jonathan shook his head. "No proof, just suspicions so far. But even if it does turn out these kids are involved, there's bigger issues at stake, and we're flat out of ideas. You worked with those inner-city youth groups, didn't you? Please, Mercy. I'd really appreciate your input."

Mercy's lips parted in astonishment. An invitation to participate in a project of supreme interest to her father, not as "Daddy's little girl" but as an adult with something to contribute? As badly as she longed to escape Travis's condemning gaze, Jonathan's overture toward a new, more mature relationship was an opportunity she couldn't pass up.

"I'll be glad to help if I can," she murmured, taking her chair as Sam and Travis reseated themselves. Encased in black denim, Travis's lean horseman's thigh was mere inches from hers, so close she could feel the heat radiating from him, and her heart thudded.

"Never underestimate the value of a fresh perspective," the judge said. Rounding his desk, Jonathan poured a cup of coffee from a loaded silver service tray and held it out to Travis to pass to Mercy.

Their fingers brushed as she took it from him, and she knew he'd done it deliberately, just to rattle her. Knowing it still didn't stop the surge of heat that started low in her belly and flowed to her extremities. But she could ignore that, too. She had to.

"Thanks," she said evenly, raising the cup to her lips.

"No problem."

His words were polite, innocuous. But the intensity of his gaze shook her to her core, evoking memories that made her blood rush shamefully. She drank the hot brew too fast, scalding her tongue.

"Careful, you'll hurt yourself," he murmured.

Eyes straight ahead, Mercy took another swallow to prove he was wrong.

Rubbing the back of his neck, Sam spoke. "I just wish there was some way to find out for sure if these boys are the ones taking our stock. We could be wasting our time on nothing. There must be a weak link somewhere."

"Chase Conly," Honey said promptly. "He's the youngest, and I think he was beginning to trust me as a friend before all this started up. But now..." She shoved her glasses to the top of her head and shrugged. "I swear he's hiding something, but I don't know what."

"I recall that hard-case uncle of his came up before my bench a few years back," the judge mused. "Assault and battery? I forget. Guess he's no help?"

Honey hesitated. "Dan Conly's about as closemouthed as Chase, so I guess it runs in the family. He's raising barrel-racing and cow ponies on a shoestring, and took his nephew in when no one else would, but *hostile* sure describes the way he treats me whenever I want to talk about Chase's problems."

"Defensiveness and overprotectiveness are qualities I typically saw in parents I dealt with," Mercy said.

"Lot of pride involved in that kind of thing," Travis drawled. "And fear."

Mercy stiffened, pricked by the hidden message in Travis's comment. Well, let him think what he would. She knew that her decision was best, the only way, in fact.

"I simply wish there was some way to reach these kids," Honey said, tugging her lip in frustration. "Money and excitement could be motivation for rustling cattle, and not a one of them thinks he could end up in jail."

"Maybe some of the task force funds could be used to hire these boys for community service projects," Mercy suggested. "Clean up Saddlebag Park or something. We had something similar going in Ft. Worth, but it could work here, too."

"Now that's an idea," Jonathan said, snapping his fingers. "Give 'em an accomplishment to point to with pride, pay 'em a little something and keep 'em out of hot water all at the same time."

"You know, that has possibilities." Honey's expression was thoughtful. "And Saddlebag Park could certainly use a renovation."

"I think we ought to pursue it," Jonathan said heartily.

"Agreed." Enthusiasm bubbling, Honey turned a twinkling smile toward Travis. "Think we could get the world champion to endorse this project? I guarantee no casts or braces will be involved this time, and the boys will love it."

Under his mustache, Travis's grin grew into something devastating to unwary female hearts. "For you, darlin', anything."

"Uh, good." Honey smiled back, looking a trifle stunned.

Out of nowhere, a pang of pure, green-eyed jealousy smacked into Mercy's middle, stealing her breath with its unexpectedness. Confused, confounded, she hid her turmoil by setting her cup on the desk.

She was a lost cause. How could she reject Travis on the one hand, then feel like clawing the eyes of another—no doubt totally innocent!—female when he focused his attention on her and called her 'darlin''? Self-loathing roiled within her like snakes, and the emotional morass she'd been holding at bay with manic and massive amounts of work surged nearly out of control. With monumental effort, she quashed it back down again.

It wasn't so much peace she found, but numbness, and she was grateful that at least for the moment she'd stopped the hurting. Her brain shied away from the word. She wasn't in pain, was she? Just conflicted with the need to move on from a relationship that could never work and put the past and Travis King firmly behind her. As soon as she accomplished that, surely the future wouldn't look so bleak.

"Couldn't we just string up a couple of these punks until they holler 'calf rope' and tell us the truth?" Sam was grumbling. "Would be a whole lot faster, maybe save us another head or two of prime stock."

Jonathan laughed at the rancher's disgruntled expression. "Somehow I don't think the constitution would allow it, Sam."

"Figured as much." Sam grinned ruefully. "Too bad. I'd sure like some answers."

"Look," Honey said, "I'll lean on Chase and some of the others and see if I can't find something out one way or the other."

"And in the meantime," Jonathan said, "maybe we can ask Mercy to get us some more details from the Ft. Worth program? We could use a good model to get off to the right start."

Holding tight to her control, Mercy kept her expression steady. "I'd be glad to, Daddy."

"When are you headed back, Mercy?" Honey asked.

"Friday." The word nearly clogged in her throat, and she saw how Travis's shoulders tensed under his ebony shirt. With forced cheerfulness, she continued. "As you can see, Daddy's on the mend—if we can keep him from doing too much too soon—and I'm chomping at the bit to get back to work. I'll contact the appropriate parties and get your information just as soon as I get home."

Honey beamed. "Well, I'm sure we all hate to see you leave, but that would be great."

Desperate to escape, Mercy glanced at her watch again. "If you'll excuse me now, I've got to get changed and out to Mrs. Rubin's."

"We're about finished here, anyway," the judge announced, and everyone rose.

Mercy almost made a clean getaway, but Travis caught her at the base of the stairs. She froze when she felt his hand on her arm, refusing to look at him.

"Let go, Travis."

His breath whispered past her ear. "We have to talk sooner or later, darlin'."

It was weariness that made the tears prickle, she told herself, nothing more. "What's the point?"

He ground out a curse. "Damn, you're a stubborn woman."

"Let go." Her voice wobbled. "I've got things to do."

"Sure." He swung her around, forcing her to look into his angry brown eyes. "Go ahead, try to fill up every minute of every hour of every day so that you don't have to think or feel or even *be*."

"I don't know what you mean."

"Sure you do. Why do you think you're running so hard?"

"I'm not—"

"Liar." He let her go, his mouth curled with contempt and pity. "All right, have it your way for now. But the truth is, if you don't rustle up the guts to give us a chance, you're always going to come up empty. And darlin', that's a helluva place to be."

His condemnation smote her like a blade, and because she was suddenly terrified that he might be right, she fled.

"You're wearing that?"

Mercy pitched her stained clothing into the laundry room adjoining the kitchen. Turning to her mother, she tried to maintain the composure she'd fought hard to win while changing upstairs.

"At least I'm clean. And Mrs. Rubin's too polite to object to jeans. I've got to go."

Working at the kitchen table, Joycelyn stuck another scarlet maple leaf into a lavish arrangement of russet and amber Thanksgiving mums and gave her daughter a pointed look. "But it's hardly professional attire."

"Leave the girl alone," Jonathan said, wandering in.

He settled into a bow-back chair and reached for the
morning paper. "She looks fine. She always does."

"Thanks, Daddy." Mercy grabbed her doctor's bag and
kissed his cheek. "And thanks for including me today. It
means a lot."

"You're the one doing us a favor, honey."

"I'll call the youth group director as soon as I get
back," she said. "But you've got to promise not to plunge
into your full workload right away."

"Like you're already trying to? We're two of a kind,
you know, and I'm living proof being a workaholic
doesn't always get you where you want to go." He looked
at her over the headlines. "Maybe the doctor ought to
follow her own advice and find a little balance in her
life?"

Travis's words echoed in her head. *Running. Empty.*
The only way she'd ever keep the confusion of feelings
that lurked beneath the surface under control would be to
plunge herself back into her work. "Easier said than done,
but I'll try," she replied lightly, lying.

Her mother knew it was pure fabrication.

"Posh. You'll be killing yourself as usual just as soon
as you hit Ft. Worth, and you'll never come visit." Joycelyn stabbed a final sprig into the bouquet with unusual
vehemence. "At least you won't have time for that rodeo
riffraff, either."

"Joy!" Jonathan slammed the paper to the table.
"That's enough."

Surprisingly, she flushed at his tone. "Just because a
mother has certain aspirations for her offspring—"

"Mercy's a grown woman, capable of making her own
decisions about the company she keeps."

Mercy gulped. "You're right, Daddy, thanks. And,
Mother, you can rest your mind on one count. I'm not

'seeing' Travis, except as an old friend. Once I'm back in Ft. Worth, I doubt if our paths will cross at all.''

"I hope it's not because of something we've said or done." The judge jammed his hands into his cardigan pockets, his expression ominous. "We were pompous fools to worry about the social standing of your friends back when you were younger."

"We were *parents,*" Joycelyn protested. "What's wrong with wanting the best for our child?"

"It was obviously a mistake not to trust Mercy's judgment. The Preston boys and Travis King were—are—fine young men. And it's high time we stopped interfering in Mercy's private life."

"I don't call a mother's concern interference, Jonathan." Features stiff, Joycelyn snatched up the flowers and stalked toward the door. "Excuse me, I've got to deliver these to the church for tonight's service."

"Mother—"

Joycelyn disappeared toward the garage, and the judge caught Mercy's eye as she took a step to follow. "No, let her go."

"She's upset."

"She'll get over it." Jonathan sighed and shook his head. "Your mother's a good woman, but you can't let anyone else's expectations keep you from finding your own path."

"I know that."

"Do you?" He took Mercy's hand. "Look, your mother loves you, only wants the best for you. But if you're happy, she'll come around, so if you've found something precious, don't let it slip through your fingers."

Mercy bit her lip to still a sudden tremor. "If it were only that simple."

"Don't waste a second chance. They're precious and

hard to come by." He winked and squeezed her hand. "I should know."

"How did you find Mrs. Rubin today?"

"She's dying."

Mercy shifted beside her mother on the crowded pew. The First Methodist church was jammed with Flat Fork citizens attending the nondenominational Thanksgiving prayer service. A mixed choir that included Roni Preston was already filing into the choir loft, and several local ministers sat in chairs behind the pulpit. Accompanied by the low tones of an organ prelude, teenage girls handed out programs printed with pumpkins and turkeys.

The scene made Mercy smile a bit and concede that Flat Fork wasn't such a bad little town. In fact, there wasn't another that fit the ideal of "home" quite so well. She wondered absently when she'd realized that.

"Well, I'm sorry to hear she's doing poorly," Joycelyn said, elegant as always in a winter white suit and pearls. "Her family?"

"They're still trying to pretend everything's going to be all right." Mercy smoothed the soft knit of her own burgundy cowl-necked dress over her knees. "Denial."

"We all handle such things in our own way," Joycelyn murmured.

Mercy nodded. As she watched latecomers file down the aisle, she thought about elderly Mrs. Rubin, frail as a bird in her sickbed, yet serene with herself and her fate and willing to let her family hold on to their illusions for as long as they needed them. "But at some point, you just got to face facts, honey," she'd said.

Mercy pressed her lips together. There was a message there, if only she could decipher it through the filter of her own riotous emotions.

A small convulsive tightening where the loose knot of her hair bared her nape made her look up, every sense alert. The warm nuances of Travis's voice came clearly to her over the murmuring congregation, lodging low and quivering in her depths. She stifled a groan. Would she never be free of this involuntary awareness, this vital connection that drew her heart despite everything her head told her?

Hoping he wouldn't spot her, she kept her eyes toward the pulpit. Dressed in suits and string ties, Travis and Sam made their way up the aisle, Sam busy juggling baby Jessie on his hip, and settled into a pew on the other side. Jessie was doing her best to divest herself of a frilly bonnet, and as Travis turned to hold the wriggling toddler so Sam could attend to her, he unhesitatingly pinned Mercy with a look over his shoulder that said that he'd not only known exactly where she sat, but also her innermost thoughts, as well as the fact that a shameful heat rushed through her blood at his merest glance.

Mercy gulped and clasped her hands in her lap just as the Methodist pastor announced the invocation and everyone rose. Beside her, Joycelyn frowned.

"Are you all right?"

"Of course." Mercy's whisper was brittle. "Why shouldn't I be?"

The pleat between her brows deepened, and Joycelyn flicked a glance at the men across the aisle, but didn't answer. The program began, but within moments Mercy was oblivious, going through the motions as the ministers gave their talks, the choir sang "Come Ye Thankful People, Come," and the collection plate for needy families went around.

Like a magnet her eyes were drawn again and again to the back of Travis's raven-dark head. His shoulders looked immensely broad under the unaccustomed jacket, the strong lines of his jaw and neck sturdy and familiar. Yearning stirred, and barriers held rigidly in place trembled and strained against a wild and terrible need.

Run, her head ordered. *Rest,* her heart whispered.

When Travis took Jessie on his knee to keep her quiet, bending his face toward hers and making her dimple, Mercy thought she would break wide open with love.

The walls fell. Denial shattered. What her father and Roni and perhaps even old Mrs. Rubin had seen and hinted at became clear as she gave up the fight at last. She was in love with Travis King, and probably had been since she was seventeen.

The knowledge brought no peace.

It changed nothing.

And it scared her spitless.

Because if she followed her heart, it was sure to be broken, and she knew that she couldn't survive that again. Mercy closed her eyes against a tidal wave of pain. He was still a tumbleweed, a live-for-the-eight-second-thrill rodeo man who'd never change.

And for all her fearless Emergency Room expertise, she was a proven coward in matters of her own heart. She knew that if she allowed herself to love Travis, it would be a full commitment, nothing held back, and then when he grew tired of her and blew on to the next lady, or when he finally ran out of luck in the rodeo arena and lost his life, she wouldn't be merely grief stricken.

It would destroy her.

"Your hands are like ice." Joycelyn took the hymnal from Mercy and shoved it into the holder on the back of the pew. "You must be coming down with something."

Mercy became aware that the service was over, the final hymn echoing in the sanctuary, people milling in the aisles. She shook her head, focusing, but nothing would clear the misery that chilled her to the bone.

"I—I guess I'm just a little tired, Mother," she murmured. Standing, she gathered her purse and coat and moved into the aisle. "It's been a long day. I'd just like to go home."

"Good evenin', ladies. Fine service, wasn't it?" Sam perched Jessie on his arm and tugged the hem of her smock over her diaper.

Travis stood at his side, his eyes heating as they moved over the curves revealed by Mercy's clinging dress. "You look beautiful tonight, darlin'."

Needle sharp, a pain throbbed behind the bridge of Mercy's nose, and her lips felt stiff. "Thank you."

"I thought the program was exceptional, Mr. Pres— Sam," Joycelyn said. Her blue eyes softened on the beguiling little redhead. "My, how she's growing."

"Like a weed." Roni joined them, still clad in her blue satin choir robe. They all moved through the crush toward the double exit doors at the rear. "Well, what did you think of the choir?"

"A bunch of veritable nightingales," Sam teased.

Laughing, Roni scooped her daughter out of his arms. The group spilled through the church entrance and onto the wide front steps choked with townspeople. The air held a winter's chill, and Mercy shrugged into her coat.

"There's coffee and some of my famous cornucopia cookies in the hall," Roni said. "Coming, anyone?"

"Actually, I told Grace Ellis I'd help serve tonight," Joycelyn replied, "but Mercedes is feeling rather fatigued. Mr. King, could I trouble you to give Mercy a lift home so that I may stay?"

Both Travis and Mercy gave her astonished looks.

"Mother, I'm fine, really—"

"Ma'am, I'd be happy to oblige—"

There was a desperate hitch to Mercy's voice. "No need for Travis to trouble himself."

His tone was rough as broken glass as he said, "No problem just as soon as I check on one thing."

"Oh, good," Joycelyn said, beaming warmly, "I'm glad that's settled."

Mercy dipped her flushed face so that only Joycelyn could hear her hiss over the general chat of the crowd. "Mother, what are you *doing?*"

The older woman's low, enigmatic murmur held both challenge and encouragement. "You'll never know for sure if you don't go, will you?"

Dumbfounded, confused by both her mother's actions and her meaning, Mercy felt Travis slip her hand through the crook of his arm.

"I'll take good care of her, Mrs. Holt," he said.

She gave him a level look. "Yes, I believe you're right."

Heart rattling in her chest, Mercy gasped softly. "Mother..."

"I'll be home after Grace and I finish in the kitchen. Don't wait up, Mercy. You know how Grace can talk." Briskly, Joycelyn turned to Roni and Sam, leading them down the sidewalk toward the brightly lit church hall. "Now what kind of cookies does our little Jessie like...?"

"I'm sorry. I don't know how you got maneuvered into this," Mercy said as Travis escorted her to his vehicle and helped her inside. Shivery and feverish at the same time, she couldn't help remembering what had taken place the last time she'd been in this truck, and she could scarcely catch her breath.

"I said it's no problem." He checked his watch, then pulled out onto the main road. "I hope you don't mind, but I promised to meet Angel Morales at my place just about now. We've moved that new bull of ours again and I want to make sure he's settled in before I head over to Deaton for Sis's holiday shindig tomorrow.''

"Trouble?"

He shrugged, his eyes fastened on the highway. "We hadn't planned on making Grenada part of the next rodeo shipment. He's wild and mean as they come, and I would have liked to work him a bit more, but we're down to just enough stock to supply a contract with the Mesquite Rodeo day after tomorrow, so we got no choice.''

"Oh. I see.''

He gave her a sharp look, and his mouth twisted. ''And you don't have to look so strung out. I'm not going to jump on you. Not without your permission.''

Electricity strummed between them. ''Good of you,'' she said, strangled.

He laughed, a harsh sound with no humor. "Oh, I'm learning my lessons the hard way. Here we are.''

They jounced up the long gravel drive into the Flying K, passed the ranch house in its shadowy shroud of leafless trees, then pulled up at the corral next to the red-painted wooden barn. Angel Morales stood beside the King and Preston cattle trailer and lifted a hand in greeting. The truck headlights cast twin beams of gold through the fence, revealing an occasional flash of buff-colored hide between the boards.

"Be right back." Opening the door, Travis went to confer with Angel.

But Mercy's attention was all on the hulking, ill-tempered animal confined in the corral. She'd rarely been this close to a bull this size, especially not one whose sole purpose in life was to stomp into pulp any arrogant cowboy who tried to ride him. Drawn by a sick fascination, Mercy slid from the truck and followed Travis.

Peeping over the top fence board, she watched the bull snort and stomp and charge around the corral. He'd evidently not taken well to being transported at this time of the night. Mucus ran from his nostrils as he hooked imaginary enemies, and the scent of warm rawhide and maddened bull slobber was musty and choking despite the chill of the night air.

Shivering, Mercy turned up her coat collar, but it wasn't the raw temperature that nipped at her. Rather, it was the stomach-churning reality she faced: that Travis took dangerous chances and made deadly choices every time he rode. And the sight of this two-thousand pounds of viciousness had brought it home to her.

Travis and Angel were still in deep conversation at the fence. Mercy turned away, a hand pressed to her fluttering belly, her mouth floating with saliva as nausea threatened. Breathing harshly, looking for refuge, she crossed to the hay-fragrant barn and slipped inside.

A security lamp on a pole outside, as well as the truck headlights, gave just enough interior light for her to stumble her way to the line of stalls. She clutched the top of one wooden gate and pressed her forehead against her clenched hands, fighting back the threatening waves of sickness and fear. She was right, she wasn't big enough or strong enough or brave enough to deal with the continual possibility that Travis's next ride could be his last. Any idiot with an ounce of self-preservation would run like hell.

Out of the darkness came the sound of Angel's truck leaving, then Travis's big Appaloosa horse whinnied a soft greeting to someone. Travis's hands found her shoulders. He tightened his fingers when he felt the shudders wracking her.

"Darlin'? God, what's wrong?"

"You. Me. This. Leave me be, Travis," she pleaded brokenly. "Have a little pity."

"I can't." His voice was thick with pain. He turned her to face him, framing her cool cheeks in his warm hands. "God help me. I just can't."

"But why?"

"Because I love you. God, are you blind?" Travis bent over her in the darkness, his dark eyes glittering with an intense and unsettling light. "I've *always* loved you. Since the first moment I clapped eyes on you. It hasn't changed for me since then. It never will."

"Oh, God." The burden of his devotion overwhelmed her, and she moaned. "What am I going to do?"

"Simple answer, darlin'. Marry me."

Nine

There. He'd done it now. Spoken too soon. Burned his bridges. Forced her into a corner. Mistake. *Disaster.*

Beneath his hands Mercy quivered like a reed in the wind, and her stricken expression struck abject fear in his heart.

"Oh, Travis..."

"Is it that unthinkable?" Throat thick, he brushed his thumb over the tremulous corner of her mouth. "To live with me, have kids, be a family?"

"You don't know what you're asking."

"I want you to be my wife." Sliding his hands to the curve of her shoulders, he bent his head and kissed her gently, a chaste pressing of lips, but with the fire of passion burning beneath the tender onslaught. She could no more hide the response that stirred within her than he could, and he smiled against her mouth, murmuring. "You know. 'Until death us do part.'"

She jerked backward against the stall gate, gasping as if she'd been punched, her voice panicky. "I can't."

He frowned. The Appaloosa stomped and blew softly behind him, and the familiar scent of hay and warm animal should have been comforting but wasn't. "Can't? Or won't?"

"It's the same."

"The hell it is."

"You know it can't work."

"That's fear speaking."

"Yes." She didn't deny it. "We can't change who we are."

"That's not what I'm asking."

"Isn't it?" Teeth chattering, Mercy folded her arms around herself, shivering under her coat. "You risk your life every time you climb into a rodeo chute and you want me just to accept that, to love you, anyway. But if I did, and I lost you—" She shook her head. "I can't do it."

"Is that all it is?" Relieved, he smiled, reaching to smooth her hair. "Don't worry, blue eyes, I can handle it."

She went very still. "But I can't. What if I asked you to give it all up? Right now, this minute?"

Travis hesitated. "Why now? It's not as though it's something I can do forever, anyway."

"You see?" Her voice cracked.

"Dammit, that's not fair."

"We're addicts, Travis, hooked on the adrenaline highs we get from our careers. I wouldn't be any happier changing mine than you would be yours."

Somehow he felt as if he'd joined her in that tight, desperate corner. He swallowed. "No, if that's what it takes—"

"Let my fear force you into a decision that isn't right

for you, then have your resentment destroy what we do have? No. I won't do that to either of us."

Bitterness swelled in his chest. "So what *do* we have, Mercy? Has it all been some sort of high school reunion game for you?"

"Oh, God, no." Choking, she took a step forward, laying her palm where his heart pounded in his chest. A single tear trail glimmered down her cheek. "I couldn't bear for you to believe that."

"Don't. You know I can't stand it when you cry. Never could. I—oh, hell."

With a groan, Travis pulled her close and covered her mouth with his. When he lifted his head, his breathing was ragged, his body aflame, his head full of half-formed apologies. One hand tangled in her chignon and the other knotted in the soft knit of her dress. He couldn't seem to unclench either fist.

And she surprised him, reaching for his face as he drew back, holding his jaw, tracing the line of his mustache with trembling fingers.

"This." Her voice was a husky pulse beat in his blood, her breath against his skin like a fever. "This is what we have, Travis."

Hope and desperation strummed within his frame, chords of a song whose ending might not yet be written. "Yes," he muttered, his tongue flicking her fingertips as they moved over his mouth.

She stretched upward against him, pressing her lips to his, and he tasted salt and sweet woman and a desperation that matched his own. Her whisper was raw with need. "All we can do is take what we've been given. Only fools ask for more."

"Then I'm a damn fool, darlin', and I'm going to do my best to make you one, too."

Scooping her up into his arms, he carried her out of the barn and into his darkened house. He only bothered with one light in the hall, hitting the switch with his elbow as he passed. Arms draped around his neck, she lay acquiescent until he set her to her feet again inside his man-tailored bedroom, then she was shrugging out of her coat, pushing off his jacket, her hands avid, her lips tracing his jawline.

Travis cupped her breasts through the clinging knit of her dress and was rewarded by her shuddering sigh. Their weight was perfection in his palms, their centers hard buttons pressing against the soft fabric, and he massaged and kneaded the pliant heaviness while he nuzzled the tender bend of her neck and his blood burned.

She found the end of his string tie and pulled it free, then tugged at his shirttail, sliding her slim fingers up the corded plane of his belly. Growling in his throat, he ripped his shirt off, then pressed the flat of her hands against his chest and took her mouth again in a drugging kiss.

Sweeping his tongue past the barrier of her lips, he tested and tasted every groove and plane, dueling wickedly. Her knees sagged, and he caught her tight, then finished what he'd started with her hair, loosing it to her shoulders and burying his fingers in the silken mass. The scent of her, all female and wildflowers and arousal, filled his senses, made him dizzy.

Feasting on her mouth, he found the zipper at her back and slipped it down her spine, teasing her with the rasp of his rope-worn fingertips against silky underthings, silkier skin. The dress slid from her shoulders, and he brushed his lips across ivory skin, smoothing the velvet of his mustache against satin, smiling as she shivered uncontrollably.

"Travis…" It was a plea and a curse.

"Ah, sweet, sweet Mercy. You turn a man every which way but loose."

The dress slipped further, dropped to the floor, and he released the clasp of her satin bra, and that vanished, too. Reverently he slid the backs of his knuckles down the slim column of her throat to rest in the hollow between her breasts, then thumbed the turgid tips. She made a sound in her throat that went straight to his throbbing loins.

Slowly, tormenting her as well as himself, he bent and licked one rosy nipple, then the other—small tastes, harbingers of more succulent fare for a connoisseur of female delights. Mercy jerked and buried her fingers in his hair as if in no other fashion could she stay upright, and she guided his hungry mouth to take her more deeply.

But he would not be rushed, not with this woman, not with so much at stake. He had to show her that he knew her, both strength and weakness, and somehow make her believe they were possible together. Reaching, he stripped her of the rest of her garments, and his heart drummed at the sight of her, soft and curved and fully revealed to him for the first time, yet mysterious still in the dim light spilling from the hallway.

"You take my breath." He sculpted her with his hands, learning every bend and turn of her body, holding her next to him and absorbing her heat.

She pressed against him, exploring his biceps, the washboard of his rib cage, nipping at his collarbone with her teeth. Impatient, she reached for his belt buckle, but he was too close already. Brushing her hands aside, he scraped back bedcovers, then lifted her and gently placed her on the ebony sheets.

She was golden hair and alabaster skin, and her pale form seemed to radiate with an inner glow against the dark cotton. He'd never seen anything so beautiful, never wanted a woman with this intensity. She was afraid that he'd die under the hooves of a bull; he was afraid he'd die if he didn't touch her in every way a man could. And he knew that would take a lifetime.

Her blue eyes were hazy as she reached for him. Kicking off boots, he stripped down to his briefs and lay beside her, shuddering when her fingertips unerringly found his bronzed male paps beneath the crisping of dark chest hair. Mouths mated, melded, and he swept his palm across her hipbones and lower, skimming belly and thighs.

Mercy moved restlessly, little whimpers of pleasure in her throat, trying to turn to meet him, but he pressed her back into the bedclothes. She retaliated by finding the indentation of his navel, then slipping fingers beneath the elastic of his briefs, cupping the steely length of his arousal with a velvet caress that nearly sent him over the edge of mindlessness.

"Not so fast," he growled, catching her hands and pressing them to the pillow beside her ears. Holding her there, he dipped his head and traced the contours of her neck with a damp tongue tip, then laved the quivering swells of her bosom with a concentration that made her squirm and protest with a gasp.

"You don't play fair."

"You know what they say about love and war."

"Which is this?"

"You decide." He caught a nipple between his teeth and tugged gently, evoking another gasp. Closing his lips around the tip, he suckled strongly. Her back arched and she cried out, a sound that was nearly a sob. He turned his attention to the other nipple, holding her helpless, using his mouth until she was writhing and moaning, swearing at him to stop, not to stop.

Releasing her hands, he moved lower, holding her hip-bones, delving into her navel with his tongue, then exploring the crisp triangular thatching of blond hair.

"Travis, no…"

"I have to." He pressed her thighs apart, overcoming her protest, her resistance no match for the quivering pleasure shaking every muscle. He tasted the dewy petals of her womanhood, giving no quarter, finding and pressing the small kernel of pulsating pleasure. Her hands clenched on his shoulders, her knees flexed, and with a high cry, she shattered for him, convulsing and arching with a series of contractions that went on and on and left her limp and gasping and Travis awed and gratified and so hard he thought he'd burst.

"Damn you," she whispered, her fingers digging into the muscles at the top of his shoulders. "Damn you, Travis King."

"Anytime, darlin'." He slid upward again, slanting his mouth over hers, letting her feel the weight of him, the way his body ached for hers.

She tugged at his briefs and he helped, kicking out of them. Kneading his hips, she traced the tendons on the backs of his thighs, then slipped her hands between their bodies and stroked him intimately. Shuddering, Travis twined his tongue with hers, stealing her breath, but she was equally relentless, urging him with lips and fingers toward madness. He cupped her mound, sliding a fingertip between passion-swollen flesh into the slick, heated passageway, knowing she was ready again by the way she quivered.

He drew back, resting on his forearms, and their gazes locked. Blue eyes met brown in an exchange of messages and rites as old as time. Wordlessly she softened, opened. Awestruck and silent, he lifted her buttocks, positioned himself, then plunged home in one powerful thrust, claiming her fully.

Travis arched his back, resting on his hands, gazing down at the place where they joined, dark to light, male to female, one flesh. "You're mine."

To prove it to her, he withdrew almost completely, teeth bared at her murmur of protest, then buried himself again in her heated depths. She welcomed him, locking her heels in the small of his back, reaching for him with a wildness to her kisses that sent him reeling. The rhythm built, a tangible force that compelled and pulled and tormented, so that when she broke again, keening his name, he exploded, as well, pouring his life and his heart and his love into his woman in a cleansing, pulsating frenzy of white-hot ecstasy that left them both shaken to the essential depths of their being.

The blood pounded in Travis's temples, coherent thought impossible as the riptides of pleasure sucked him under, but he knew he'd never experienced anything to equal this, never thought in all of his godforsaken life to feel anything so right and good. Tightening his arms around her as oblivion overtook him, he prayed that she would know it, too.

A pale Thanksgiving dawn gleamed through the dusting of frost on the window panes, revealing masculine, oak bedroom furnishings, forest green, khaki and ebony linens, and a small brown plastic bottle of prescription pain relievers on the nightstand. The room was pleasantly warm with central heating, but Mercy shivered, reminded forcefully of the choices made by the man with the tantalizing black mustache who slept so deeply beside her. Reality was an unwelcome intruder after the passion they'd shared throughout the night, and helpless, and too weak for the moment to do anything else, Mercy lingered in a realm where denial was still possible, snuggling closer to share Travis's heat under the covers.

Watching him breathe.

Selfishly storing up memories.

Pretending.

What would it be like to wake up beside this man for the rest of her life? To have the right to reach for him whenever she wanted? To love him freely, without fear?

The fantasy was too sweet, too tempting. The impossibility an agony that sliced like a knife blade through the fragile tissue of heart and soul. She closed her eyes on a billow of pain.

"Don't, darlin'." Rough fingertips stroked the hair at her temple. Then he gathered her close, bare limbs tangling under the bedclothes, naked bodies a perfect fit of lush curves and hard angles. "I don't ever want you to wake up beside me crying."

Lifting her eyes, she raised trembling fingers, touching his lips, exploring the softness of his mustache. "I know. And I'm not crying."

Yet.

His brows drew together in a straight line. "You're still scared. It's too soon for you to talk about marriage. I shouldn't have pushed—"

It was old territory, ground she couldn't bear to cover again, so she kissed him to stop his words, pressing him back against the pillows and climbing on top of him. She touched him everywhere, her hands avid on his muscular shoulders and pebbled nipples, her mouth teasing his lips, then exploring the line of his strong jaw and the cords of his neck. He stiffened with surprise and pleasure, hands flattening convulsively against her back.

When she moved lower, finding the dip of his navel,

Travis jerked. She went lower still, touching her tongue to the burgeoning heat of him.

His hands clenched in her hair. "What are you doing?"

Loving you.

She wanted to give him everything, but she couldn't. So this was a gift, something for him to remember her by. Only selfishly, she knew she'd gain more than she gave. She closed her lips around him.

The groan that tore from his throat was deep and heartfelt. Feeling powerful, she tormented and tantalized, pushing him toward forgetfulness as he'd pushed her time and again. But close to the summit, he denied her the final joy. Rolling from her with a primal growl, he rose to the bedside and swung her across his lap, pinning her with one hand at her nape and ravaging her mouth mercilessly.

In the next moment he lifted her to straddle him, impaling her powerfully, completely, and Mercy cried out at the arrow-swift and liquid plunge of pleasure that seared her nerves and steamed her blood. Hand to the small of her back, lips to the rosy, pointed crests of her breasts, he arched her backward, pressing them together where they joined, spiraling and tightening the quickening of their desire to unendurable limits.

Head thrown back, storm tossed, Mercy clung to him, riding the waves of delight, knowing what he wanted to prove to her, knowing it was transient and impossible, and yet for this moment unable to deny that this—*this*—was all that mattered in their tiny corner of the possible universe.

A universe that exploded, contracted, grew light and dark, and took her to a plane of existence without bounds and beyond experience. Gasping, tumbling heavenward, she threw herself into the wildness, felt her body clench and heard Travis groan her name as he followed into the pulsating radiance.

As shooting stars are wont, they eventually burned out and fell to earth. Limp and weeping, Mercy lay against the tumbled covers, Travis's dark head pressed to her breast. She was on fire and icy all at once, overwhelmed by both pleasure and imminent loss. His ragged breaths wafted too hot across her flushed skin, burning her with guilt and remorse and grief.

"We can take it as slow as you want, darlin'." The desperate despair in his voice smote her and she trembled.

"It would kill us both."

He was silent a long time. "I reckon this isn't enough, is it?"

After this glimpse of paradise, this tantalizing promise of what they might have had together...? If only they weren't who they were. If only the fear and the risks and the choices they made wouldn't eventually totally destroy their rocky relationship.... They would end ultimately in bitterness and hatred, and to Mercy that would be the most unendurable tragedy of all, worse even than death. She touched his hair with loving fingers, and hot tears trickled toward her ears.

"No." She choked. "And you deserve more."

"Mercy—"

"Leave it be, cowboy. Some things we just can't fix, no matter how much we want to."

His lips moved against her flesh in a silent, grinding curse. A heated drop of moisture landed between her breasts. Shocked, she stopped breathing. Unthinkably, the man who denied pain and defied death shook like a babe in her arms. Pressing her mouth to the top of his dark head, she held him for the last time and they both cried.

* * *

"There's more sweet potato pie."

Mercy set her cup and saucer in the kitchen sink and glanced at her mother. "Thanks, but I couldn't possibly."

In an autumn-colored silk dress, Joycelyn tore off a piece of plastic wrap and tucked it around the pie plate. "You hardly ate a thing at dinner."

"It was a lovely Thanksgiving meal despite my lack of appetite. You and Daisy outdid yourselves." She cocked an ear at the crowd noises coming from the den where Jonathan was snoozing in front of the afternoon's TV football games. "And I don't think Daddy even noticed that everything on the menu was low fat and heart wise."

"Oh, he noticed, all right." Joycelyn's smile was dry. "But he knows better than to complain. He's taken his new regimen to heart, thanks to you, and I think he'll stick to it."

Mercy stuck her hands in the pockets of powder blue wool slacks that matched her silky blouse. The dressy outfit was not so much a concession to holiday spirit as armor. "Good. I intend to have you both around for a long time."

Joycelyn placed the pie in the refrigerator, then hesitated. "I know the past few weeks have been...difficult, but I want you to know how much I've appreciated your being here. Are you all right?"

Mercy shrugged and brushed her hair back from her shoulders. "Sure. Why?"

"You look tired. And I didn't hear you come in last night."

"It was late." Her throat tightened involuntarily, and she pressed her lips together in a caricature of a smile. "In fact, I'm way behind schedule, and I've got packing to finish if I'm to get an early start tomorrow, so—"

Worry and concern warming her eyes, Joycelyn crossed the kitchen and gave her daughter a thorough hug. "You don't have to explain. I just want you to be happy."

Startled and moved by her mother's unaccustomed display of affection, Mercy swallowed hard. "I know that, Mom."

"And whatever you choose, I'll support. Your father isn't the only one who can learn something out of all this."

"Yes. Thank you." A wordless understanding and acknowledgment of their love for each other passed between them, and Mercy had to clear her throat of a lump of emotion before she could speak again. "I've decided something, too."

"What's that?"

"I'm not going to accept as much call from now on, and I'm going to come home to visit more regularly, I promise. You and Daddy can plan a trip or two my way, too. I'll get theater tickets or something...."

"We'd like that. A lot." Joycelyn smiled, then touched Mercy's loose hair, flicking it with her fingers. "This looks nice. Are you sure I can't get you that pie?"

"I'm sure." Mercy shook her head, smiling despite an emotional prickle of tears. The man she loved was lost to her, and she was feeling fragile and lost, but it seemed the Lord was opening the door to another important relationship, and she was grateful.

"Then I suppose I'd better go see if the Aggies have your father cursing or cheering," her mother said with a wry twist of her lips. "Why don't you join us? That packing can wait."

"You're right. I—" The kitchen phone rang. "Go ahead. I'll get it."

Joycelyn disappeared toward the den as Mercy reached for the receiver. ''Hello?''

It was Honey Jones, sounding uncertain and awkward over the lines. ''Uh, does Travis happen to be there?''

Mercy winced at the jolt Travis's name produced, but forced herself to keep her tone even. ''No. I believe he was going to his sister's in Deaton for the holiday.''

''Oh, damn! And Sam's at his in-laws in Austin.''

A trickle of alarm skittered down Mercy's spine. ''What's up?''

''Well, nothing, maybe. But I just got a call from a sister of one of our boys. She overheard some talk makes me certain these kids are rustling King and Preston's stock.''

Mercy twisted the curly phone cord around her finger. ''Well, good. Maybe you can put a stop to it now.''

''Only problem is her brother's vanished. She's convinced they're up to no good right this very minute.''

''In broad daylight? Surely not.''

''That's what I said, but if somehow they got wind that both Sam and Travis are out of pocket...''

A frown puckered Mercy's brow. ''You called the sheriff?''

''Everyone's working a big wreck out on the interstate. Could be a while before a patrol car's free.''

''And Travis just moved their prize bull to the Flying K last night. They could go bust if they lose Grenada.'' Chewing her lip, Mercy made an impulsive decision. ''Tell you what, I'll ride out there right now and take a look. If there's some activity going on, these kids won't dare try anything.''

''You don't mind?''

''Of course not.'' It was a final favor for Travis, concerning something crucial in his life, one last thing she could do to show she cared. After the disappointment she'd been to him, she welcomed the opportunity, little enough that it was.

Relief colored Honey's voice. "And I'll make a run past the Lazy Diamond. It's probably a false alarm, but if you see anything, just stay out of it. Those older boys can be mean and unpredictable."

"Nothing I haven't handled a hundred times during a typical night in the E.R.," Mercy said dryly.

"Just be careful."

"Sure. What could happen?"

Ten

Hell could break loose. And it had.

Tearing down the lane toward the Flying K in her convertible, Mercy absorbed in one astonished and horrified glance the old truck and battered horse trailer centered in the open corral gate, the trio of shouting, lasso-waving boys and the enraged two-ton bull they were attempting to load.

Disaster and death on four hooves.

Her heart leapt to her throat. Rustling was a crime of little significance if the lawbreakers were dead.

No other vehicles sat in the ranch house drive. A cold wind blustered through the bare-branched cottonwoods and twirled adobe-colored dust in lonely whirlwinds across the sun-spilled work yard. She was on her own.

Skidding the car to a shuddering halt on the loose gravel beside the corral, she vaulted from the seat, pounding for the fence.

"Damn it! I said get behind the sumbitch!"

A hulking pug-faced teenager in a corduroy jacket stood protected behind the open trailer gate, gesturing and cursing at his younger companions to herd the beast inside. Chase Conly and another boy not much older nervously closed in at mid-corral behind a snorting, stamping Grenada, whose mean, beady eyes focused for the moment on the leader of this rag-tag outlaw gang.

Mercy clambered up the fence railing. "Are you out of your minds? Get out of there!"

Three panicked faces turned her way.

"Oh, sh—" The pug-faced kid bolted for the truck door. The other two boys scattered in opposite directions. Grenada snorted, spun, chose a new target and charged after Chase.

Dimly, Mercy sensed when the third youngster tumbled into the safety of the pickup's bed. The older culprit gunned the vehicle into life, and the two abandoned their friend to his fate, squealing through the gate in high gear with the trailer bouncing like a rubber ball behind them. But Mercy's terrified gaze locked on the slender, dark-headed youth sprinting for his life on the other side of the enclosure.

Knuckles white on the top rail, she screamed. *"Run!"*

He nearly made it.

Chase's boot hit the first rail of the fence, then the second, but Grenada was on him, swinging his massive head like a battering ram, scraping his pointed horns at the irritating interloper clawing up the boards. The boy went flying, spread-eagled and spinning through the air like a human Frisbee. He landed in the center of the corral with a sickening thud and didn't move. The bull paused, apparently puzzled that his quarry had vanished.

"Oh, God!" Every lifesaving instinct Mercy possessed

kicked into automatic. Without thinking, she scrambled over the top of the fence and raced toward the immobile, defenseless boy.

Perhaps it was her gasping breaths or the vibration of her shoes on the earth that turned his attention, but Grenada wheeled. With a snort that sprayed hot saliva, the bull charged again—straight at the fallen boy.

Mercy ran at him, slipping out of her jacket, yelling and waving it until the raging creature caught the movement and turned his head. Desperately she tossed the jacket in the opposite direction.

The bull almost bought it. He trotted two steps after the fluttering garment, then thought better of it, swinging back, ducking his head and galloping straight at Mercy.

Terrified, she dodged by instinct alone, but she wasn't fast enough. The impact as the animal roared past flung her to her knees, and a fiery pain tore into her right arm, nearly blinding her with the intensity of the agony. From a great distance she thought she heard a shout.

Then Grenada was coming back at her again, sharp, evil hooves grinding dust in a deadly tattoo, and beside her in the dirt Chase moaned, helpless. Throwing herself down over the injured boy, Mercy braced herself as death thundered toward them.

"What the hell?"

Wrenching his steering wheel, Travis barely missed being run off his own driveway by the battered pickup truck and empty trailer barreling past him like a bat out of Hades. He got a glimpse of a pug-faced boy he recognized. The implications made his sister's turkey dinner curdle in his gut, but his automatic curse never made it past his lips because at that moment he spotted Mercy's red convertible beside Grenada's corral, and hot dread splashed over him.

Something was very, very wrong.

He was out of the truck before it stopped rolling, running for the corral, vaulting the fence like a hurdler, his heart in his mouth, injuries and stiffness forgotten in the rush of adrenaline. He saw it all in stop-action shots.

The awkward, unnatural sprawl of the motionless boy.

Grenada, horns tucked and charging with vicious and murderous intent.

The blood.

The blonde.

And then she did the most incredible thing and threw herself over the boy and directly into Grenada's deadly track.

"No!" Abject terror turned his veins to icicles. Everything operated in slow motion. Invisible quicksand dragged at his heels. He sank in a sea of desperation.

It took an eternity. It took the barest atomic flicker of a second. In that increment of time, Travis took whatever hope he had of heaven and bartered it for life—hers.

He stepped into Grenada's path.

As if conjured by the devil himself, the man in black materialized between her and the charging demon. Mercy thought she'd been filled to the brim with terror before, but cascades of new fear flooded her. Travis!

Boots spread, he bounced slightly on the balls of his feet, mere feet—inches!—from slashing horns. And then he actually caught those horns in his hands and Mercy's heart stopped beating altogether.

With an agile twist of his body, Travis faked to the right and then dodged left, missing being torn open by those razor-sharp horns by the breadth of a whisker. But he'd accomplished his purpose, and Grenada spun right, away from where Mercy lay pressed over the boy. To her horror, Travis sprinted in a circle behind the animal, coming up again in full front view of the frustrated beast to draw his attention.

Throat full of dry dust, Mercy couldn't even croak a protest. But Travis made it look deceptively easy, standing his ground again until the heart-wrenching last second, then making another leg-lifting fake that sent Grenada charging through the open gate into the barnyard while the bull rider dodged to safety in the other direction.

Light-headed with relief and loss of blood, Mercy ignored the stabbing pain in her right arm and struggled to her knees, already examining and assessing the unconscious boy's condition, using her one good hand. Travis shoved the gate shut, a precaution lost on the bull whose gallop became a totally disinterested, indolent amble down the driveway fence row as he picnicked on a few late-growing sprigs of grass.

Then Travis was beside her, his face pasty white. He whipped a bandana out of his pocket, pressing it to the crimson tide that soaked her silky blue shirtsleeve and dripped off her fingertips. His voice shook. "Oh, Jesus, darlin'."

"I'm not that bad." She assessed Chase's pulse, lifted an eyelid. Though her own eyes were pain darkened, her words were clipped, competent, in charge. "Fetch my bag out of the car and call for the medivac chopper. This boy's in trouble."

The comfortable patient room at Ft. Worth's John Peter Smith Hospital was peaceful and dim, illuminated only by the golden bars of afternoon sunshine slanting from between the slats of the miniblind at the single window. An

electronic IV apparatus on a pole beside the bed blinked
red numerals and beeped quietly. A turquoise plastic water pitcher and tumbler sat on the nightstand. The nurse's
call button and the television remote control lay neatly
clipped to the pristine white pillowcase with a chrome
pincher.

It was a setup guaranteed to facilitate each patient's full
and complete recovery. And after two days of it, Dr.
Mercy Holt was going completely out of her mind.

For the hundredth time in the past hour, Mercy shot an
impatient glare at the IV monitor connected to the tube in
her arm. The wound Grenada had given her had been a
dirty one, requiring extensive lavage, twenty-one stitches
and a round of IV antibiotics. She couldn't protest the
regimen or even being admitted, not when the use of her
arm was at stake and the treatment was exactly what she
would have recommended, anyhow.

Meanwhile she'd taken a lot of ribbing from a steady
round of hospital and E.R. staff. Some had teasingly ac-
cused her of staging her aerial grand entrance just to return to her home turf in royal style. Others averred this
was just a ploy on her part to take a few more days off—
"Gored by a bull, who did she think she was kidding?"—
and demanded she come back to work immediately, injured on not, because the E.R. just hadn't been the same
without her.

At least, Mercy thought, it was nice to know she'd been
missed these past weeks. Still, as soon as this last IV bag
of medication had run its course, she was going to demand
release and check herself out.

Sighing, favoring her bandaged arm, she used the button on the railing to crank herself to a more upright position, then settled back against the pillow. It certainly
gave one a different perspective, seeing things from this

side of the bed. From the moment when she'd become not only the attending physician but the second evacuation patient on the medivac flight from the Flying K into one of Ft. Worth's best trauma centers, things had taken on a whole new light.

From her own stretcher, she'd directed the EMTs as they worked frantically on the boy, but despite everything they'd done, Chase Conly now languished unconscious with a broken arm and head injuries in the ICU. After what they'd shared, she had a proprietary interest in the boy, and her inability to check on him in person added another level to her discontent and frustration.

Trying to get comfortable, Mercy punched her pillow and tugged her flowered hospital gown over her knees. Joycelyn had brought her an entire wardrobe of silky nightwear, but Mercy had to admit these cotton garments were more practical than sexy lingerie for changing dressings and bed baths. Travis was right, however. They were awfully drafty.

The ache in her arm moved to the region of her heart. She hadn't seen him since the ranch, and the last ghastly glimpse of his white face as the chopper had taken off haunted her. There was so much she needed to think about, to say to him, and here she sat, tied to this blasted IV line—

A soft tap at the door interrupted her turbulent thoughts. The initial sight of a familiar black cowboy hat sent her heart soaring into pounding, free-wheeling overdrive. But it was a tall stranger who hesitated in the doorway, and bitter disappointment plunged her back to earth.

"Dr. Holt?" In chambray shirt and worn denim jacket, the big man had shaggy black hair and a voice raspy with fatigue and strain. He held his hat awkwardly in his hands, as if he weren't accustomed to such courtesies, especially in front of a woman whose tumbled locks and rumpled gown made her look much younger than her profession suggested. His hard, craggy features were shadowed by a two-day growth of stubble that gave him the air of an outlaw, a haggard and rather alarming desperado. "I'm sorry to disturb you. I'm Dan Conly, Chase's uncle."

Mercy sat up straighter, gestured him to the side of the bed. "Mr. Conly, come in, please. How is Chase?"

"He came out of the coma just a little while ago. They think he's going to be fine."

"Oh, I'm so glad." Relief and satisfaction warmed her smile to the brilliance of a sunrise.

"I wanted you to know. I wanted to thank you." Dan Conly swallowed, and his Adam's apple bobbed. "They told me how you risked your own life to protect him and that if you hadn't been right there every step of the way, he might not have even made it to the hospital. I'm grateful, ma'am. More than I can say."

"No thanks necessary, Mr. Conly. I only did what I thought was right. And I'm thrilled Chase is going to recover. I know you must have been very worried."

"We're the only family either of us have left. The damn fool kid was trying to protect me." Exasperation and a hint of pride colored his gruff tone. "I've had a brush or two with the law, ma'am, and the older boys told him they'd make it look like I was involved in their rustling if he didn't help. Promised to send me to jail, him back to foster care—and he bought it. Hell of a mess."

"That kind of loyalty is rare, Mr. Conly. Chase must love you a great deal."

Dan Conly coughed and cleared his throat. Mercy pretended she didn't see the gleam of ragged emotion in his eyes. For a man such as this, it would be too embarrassing.

"I hope you can get everything straightened out," she murmured.

He shuffled his booted feet and shoved on his hat, recovering. "That Ms. Jones is going to help. Something about extenuating circumstances. And, ma'am, if there's *ever* anything I can do to repay you—"

"Just take care of that boy." She held out her hand.

Dan Conly shook it gingerly, as if she were made of porcelain, then backed toward the door. "Thank you again."

"Let me know how things go. And good luck."

Nodding, he touched the brim of his hat, then threw open the door and strode purposefully out into the corridor. Thoughtful, Mercy gazed out the window as the door drifted shut behind him. Maybe the Conly men could find their path now. She hoped so. A tickle on the back of her neck and the absence of the usual "snick" of the latch jerked her attention to the man in black filling up the doorway.

"Let you out of my sight a minute," Travis complained softly, "and already you've got gentleman callers out the wazoo."

She caught her breath. After coming so close to death—both his and her own—there wasn't anything left in her but honesty. "You're the only gentleman caller I'm interested in. Where the hell have you been, cowboy?"

That knocked the cockiness out of his half smile. He straightened from his slouch. "As soon as I heard you were okay, out running the roads fetching back King and Preston stock from a dirty, low-down yahoo by the name of Buzz Henry. The sorry so-and-so put those kids up to the whole thing."

"You're joking."

"You can't get prison time in Texas for rustling anymore, but that sucker will either be under the jail or out of business by the time Sam and I get done with him.''

She arched an eyebrow to cover her nervousness. ''So business is back on track, and you thought you'd look in on the convalescent? How very kind.''

''You make me feel as guilty as a snot-nosed kid with his hand caught in the cookie jar, Miss Mercy.'' Dark eyes smoldering and uncertain, he pushed the door completely shut and came to the side of the bed. Setting his hat aside, he picked up her hand and brushed her fingertips across his mustache, murmuring. ''For a gorgeous lady doc, who, as we say on the suicide circuit, 'smelt the slobber,' you don't look too bunged up. You really all right? Hurting anywhere?''

Rattled by his seductive gesture, she shook her head. ''Not too badly. Gives me new respect for all the times you've taken a licking, though.''

''Just as soon have spared you the experience.'' His fingers tightened on hers, and his jaw worked. ''I wanted to come sooner, I just wasn't sure you'd see me, darlin'.''

''The man who saved my life? Surely you could have guessed I'd have one of two things to say to you. Starting with thanks.''

''It's not your gratitude I want,'' he growled, his thumb rubbing the pocket of her palm.

She shivered at his touch. ''You've got it, anyway.'' And so much more.

''I'm just glad I showed up when I did. Risking your life like that for that kid.'' He shook his head in disbelief. ''You scared me out of ten years' growth. I never really understood until that moment what it felt like to have someone you love taking a life-or-death risk before your very eyes and not to be able to do a damn thing.''

"And now you do." Her voice was soft, her eyes cautious.

"And now I do. Seeing you hurt just about killed me. As feelings go, it ain't worth a damn."

"No, it's not."

"So I understand better, darlin'." Pain creased his features and darkened his eyes to polished onyx. "I don't like your decision any more than I did before, but I've been an arrogant galoot not to honor your feelings and I'm sorry. I just wish...hell, you know."

His words spread a gratifying warmth through her chest, and she touched his cheek. "May I ask you something?"

"Sure, anything."

"If you had it to do over, would you still bullfight Grenada to save me? Maybe even knowing this time you wouldn't be so lucky?"

He looked shocked. "Hell, yes."

"And I wouldn't change what I did for Chase. I wasn't being brave, just doing what I had to. I understand things like that better now, too." She took a deep breath. "So if we're both going to take the risks, anyway, maybe we should take them together?"

Travis's expression narrowed. "What are you saying?"

"That the worst feeling I ever had was thinking we might both die in that corral and knowing my fear had deprived us of whatever time we could have had together." Eyes enormous, she took the greatest risk of her life. "And that I'd never told you how much I love you, Travis King."

"Oh, darlin'." Hands trembling, Travis cupped her face, kissed her tenderly with reverence. "You think I don't know?"

"Pretty obvious, huh? Since I was seventeen."

He eased a hip onto the bed, facing her, and his tone was suddenly rough, almost angry. "So how come two people who care this much about each other are ending up apart?"

She placed her hands over his, holding the rope-toughened palms against her cheeks, and her throat swelled with emotion. "I've been so frightened."

"I know."

"But all this woke me up, Travis. What you did in that corral terrified and amazed me. You know what you're up against, you weigh your limits, and you do your job. I was wrong to doubt you."

"But it's understandable, darlin'." His mouth twisted. "I'd be the first to admit riding bulls isn't the sanest thing a man ever did."

"Well, it proved to me life is too precious to waste, and not being a part of yours scares me more than anything." A crystal teardrop leaked from the corner of her eye, and her voice shook. "If I haven't ruined it, if you'll still have me, do you think we can find a way to make it work?"

"*If?* Mercy, you're everything I've ever dreamed of." Hope, elation and desire flared behind his eyes, made his words rumble low with emotion. "And I think two smart people who love each other can do anything they damn well please."

Leaning close, he brushed his mouth to the corner of her eye, capturing the tear, then let his lips drift to the trembling corner of her mouth. "Including finding a road we can travel together. Your work—"

"—can be just as exciting in Flat Fork as here." Drawing back slightly, she gave a wry grimace and lifted her bandaged arm. "And I've got the proof."

Chuckling, he brushed his thumb over her cheekbone,

then slipped his hand to caress her neck beneath the burnished honey of her hair. "Uh-oh. Why doesn't that reassure me?"

"Maybe for the same reason discovering the most recent thing we have in common is our pain medication?"

Amused, he lifted one dark eyebrow to an inquiring angle. "So we have our work cut out for us?"

She shrugged. "When haven't we? But facing whatever comes together? I've been too busy fighting my feelings to consider it might make things easier, not harder."

"My mama always talks about love dividing the trouble and doubling the happiness."

Regret turned her lips down at the corners. "I only wish I could have seen it sooner."

"Maybe it's been a long time coming for us," he agreed solemnly. "But God knows all those years and heartaches earned us the right to a second chance."

"I guess we had to do some serious growing up, quit trying to prove something to the world, and concentrate on what's inside."

"You're a smart lady, blue eyes."

"And you're a smooth-talkin' ladies' man, Travis King, because we both know I'm a stubborn heifer. But when I'm taught a lesson, it sticks." She took a tremulous breath. "And loving you is worth any risk. Hope you're ready. I'm going for it."

His wide smile lifted his mustache, and his eyes gleamed. "Now that's the way I like to hear you talk, sweet Mercy. Come here, darlin'."

Mindful of her injured arm and the IV, he lay down beside her on the narrow bed, carefully gathering her close to his heart.

Sighing, Mercy snuggled against him. "The nurse will have a fit when she sees your dirty boots on this bed."

"Let her. Some things a man just has to do when he tells his woman he loves her. And I adore you, darlin'. Always have, always will."

She reached to stroke the dark hair at his nape, her eyes soft with love. "Me, too, cowboy."

With one hand exploring the curve of her waist, Travis slanted his mouth over hers and kissed her, deeply, sweetly, with a heart full of passion and promise and commitment. They were both breathing hard when he lifted his head again, and he groaned in frustration.

"How long you going to be tethered to this dad-blamed contraption?"

"Not much longer."

"Good, I'll spring you from this joint, and we'll find someplace to be alone where we can have a serious discussion about our future."

She plucked open the pearl snap of his black shirt and slipped her fingers inside to stroke his broad chest. "Actually, I already had someplace in mind."

Distracted, he nibbled at her ear. "Hmm?"

"For our honeymoon."

He drew back, grinning. "Going to make an honest man of me, are you?"

"At the earliest opportunity, cowboy," she said severely. "'Love'em-and-Leave'em' King goes into retirement, and I'd better not hear any objections!"

"No, ma'am. Not a one." He shivered as she continued to explore the flat planes of his chest, and his tone took on a strangled quality. "So, where do you want to go for this honeymoon?"

Mercy bit her lip, gathered her courage and looked the man she loved straight in the eye. "Las Vegas."

Travis jerked in surprise. "Tacky, glittery, not-your-style-at-all kind of town like that?"

"It has its attractions."

"Such as?"

"You and the National Rodeo Finals."

He went very still. "You mean it?"

Nodding, she moved her mouth over his, casting her love and her courage and her heart into the arena of their new life together.

"Darlin'," she drawled, "it's high time I saw you ride. I'm going to cheer you straight to the championship. You'll win, I know it."

A wonderful tenderness filled his expression, and as he bent his head to kiss her again, his voice was husky with love.

"Darlin', I already have."

Epilogue

"Trick or treat, darlin'."

Mercy came up short in the doorway of her office at Flat Fork Hospital, eyeing the lean man stretched out in her big leather chair with his boots propped on her cluttered desk top.

"Treat, definitely," she said. "Got an appointment, cowboy?"

Travis's wicked grin lifted his mustache. "I know the management personally."

"I'll say." With an air of great purpose, Mercy pushed the office door shut, dropped the final patient chart on top of a pile, then straddled the lap of her husband of nearly a year and proceeded to ravish his willing mouth. Her breathing was uneven when she drew back. "Welcome home. I didn't expect you this soon."

"We wrapped the taping early."

He nuzzled her neck, then reached under the starched

cotton of her doctor's jacket to explore her curves through the blue knit of her dress. Mercy pressed wantonly against him, her hem bunching rather immodestly about her stocking-clad thighs, to their mutual delight.

"Had a good shoot?" she asked breathlessly.

"Easy as pie. Who'd have ever thought they'd pay me good money just to talk over the TV?"

"You're good at it." Grinning, she let her fingers travel down to the saucer-sized trophy belt buckle at his waist, teasing him, stroking the metal sinuously, then letting her touch drift down the placket of his jeans where a telltale bulge leapt to life. "Nobody knows more about color commentary and rodeo than Travis King, that sweet-talkin', three-time world champion bull rider."

He stifled a groan of pleasure. "Retired."

"You're sure?"

"No regrets, darlin'. Got enough on my plate with the stock company and now this TV deal. And it spoils a man not to have to eat painkillers by the handful and walk like I'm eighty."

"No more trouble from that leg?"

"Nary a twinge."

She settled more fully against him, bent and drew her tongue over the edge of his mustache. "Good. I have plans for that leg tonight."

Travis chuckled, riding his palms up her thighs. "God, I love homecomings! Are you finished here?"

"Uh-huh, and am I ever glad. And I thought Ft. Worth had loonies on Halloween. All of Flat Fork's bats hit the belfries today."

"Never a dull moment?"

Eyes sparkling, she reached up and released the knot in her hair, shaking it down to her shoulders. "No, and I love it. Taking over the family practice from Doc Hazelton was the best move I ever made.''

"Besides marrying me.''

She gave a sultry laugh. "Fishing for compliments, cowboy?''

"You might say you missed me,'' he mock-complained.

Linking her arms around his neck, she rocked them back in the chair and kissed him until they were both dizzy. "How's that?''

With a low growl he cupped her hips beneath her skirt, then gave a grunt of pleasure when he discovered a lacy garter belt and little else. His grin got wider. "I'm glad no one but me guesses what the sexy doc has under her lab coat. Celebrating the return of your hero, are you, blue eyes?''

"Among other things,'' she murmured. "There's a treat for you in my right pocket.''

His hands flexed on her thighs. "I'm perfectly content where I am.''

"Just get it,'' she said, laughing.

Grumbling, Travis delved into her coat pocket and retrieved a small pink slip of paper, glancing at it curiously. "You know this medical stuff is Greek to me, so...''

He broke off, his eyes widening, and his boots hit the floor so fast he nearly dumped them both before he recovered and pulled Mercy into a sitting position on his lap.

"P-positive?'' he croaked.

"Uh-huh.''

"A baby? Us? Sure. Can't let the Prestons get ahead of us, can we?''

She smiled and touched his cheek. "Come summer. Just like a proper rancher's wife.''

"Thank God there's nothing proper about you, Miss Mercy."

"I knew you'd be happy."

"Darlin', I'm delirious. You, now a family of our own—God, I love you." Bending her over his arm, he kissed her thoroughly.

She sighed against his lips. "I think this could be what started all the commotion in the first place. Could you do that again, cowboy?"

"My pleasure, darlin'." He grinned. "Now latch that door and watch this rodeo get completely out of hand."

*　*　*　*　*

In April 1997
Bestselling Author

takes her Family Circle series to new heights with

In April 1997 Dallas Schulze brings readers a
brand-new, longer, out-of-series title featuring the
characters from her popular Family Circle miniseries.

When rancher Keefe Walker found Tessa Wyndham he
knew that she needed a man's protection—she was
pregnant, alone and on the run from a heartless past.
Keefe was also hiding from a dark past...but in one
overwhelming moment he and Tessa forged a family
bond that could never be broken.

Available in April wherever books are sold.

Take 4 bestselling love stories FREE

Plus get a FREE surprise gift!

Special Limited-time Offer

Mail to Silhouette Reader Service™

3010 Walden Avenue
P.O. Box 1867
Buffalo, N.Y. 14240-1867

YES! Please send me 4 free Silhouette Desire® novels and my free surprise gift. Then send me 6 brand-new novels every month, which I will receive months before they appear in bookstores. Bill me at the low price of $2.90 each plus 25¢ delivery and applicable sales tax, if any.* That's the complete price and a savings of over 10% off the cover prices—quite a bargain! I understand that accepting the books and gift places me under no obligation ever to buy any books. I can always return a shipment and cancel at any time. Even if I never buy another book from Silhouette, the 4 free books and the surprise gift are mine to keep forever.

225 BPA A3UU

Name		(PLEASE PRINT)	
Address		Apt. No.	
City		State	Zip

This offer is limited to one order per household and not valid to present Silhouette Desire® subscribers. *Terms and prices are subject to change without notice.
Sales tax applicable in N.Y.

DES-693

©1990 Harlequin Enterprises Limited

National Bestselling Author

MARY LYNN BAXTER

"Ms. Baxter's writing…strikes every chord within the
female spirit."
—Sandra Brown

LONE STAR Heat

SHE is Juliana Reed, a prominent broadcast journalist whose
television show is about to be syndicated. Until the murder…

HE is Gates O'Brien, a high-ranking member of the
Texas Rangers, determined to forget about his ex-wife. He's
onto something bad….

Juliana and Gates are ex-spouses, unwillingly involved in an
explosive circle of political corruption, blackmail and murder.

In order to survive, they must overcome the pain of the past…and
the very demons that drove them apart.

Available in September 1997 at your favorite retail outlet.

As seen on TV!
Free Gift Offer

With a Free Gift proof-of-purchase from any Silhouette® book,
you can receive a beautiful cubic zirconia pendant.

This gorgeous marquise-shaped stone is a genuine cubic
zirconia—accented by an 18" gold tone necklace.

(Approximate retail value $19.95)

Send for yours today...
compliments of *Silhouette*®

To receive your free gift, a cubic zirconia pendant, send us one original proof-of-purchase, photocopies not accepted, from the back of any Silhouette Romance™, Silhouette Desire®, Silhouette Special Edition®, Silhouette Intimate Moments® or Silhouette Yours Truly™ title available in February, March and April at your favorite retail outlet, together with the Free Gift Certificate, plus a check or money order for $1.65 U.S./$2.15 CAN. (do not send cash) to cover postage and handling, payable to Silhouette Free Gift Offer. We will send you the specified gift. Allow 6 to 8 weeks for delivery. Offer good until April 30, 1997 or while quantities last. Offer valid in the U.S. and Canada only.

Free Gift Certificate

Name: _____

Address: _____

City: _____ State/Province: _____ Zip/Postal Code: _____

Mail this certificate, one proof-of-purchase and a check or money order for postage and handling to: SILHOUETTE FREE GIFT OFFER 1997. In the U.S.: 3010 Walden Avenue, P.O. Box 9077, Buffalo NY 14269-9077. In Canada: P.O. Box 613, Fort Erie, Ontario L2Z 5X3.

FREE GIFT OFFER
084-KFD
ONE PROOF-OF-PURCHASE

To collect your fabulous FREE GIFT, a cubic zirconia pendant, you must include this original proof-of-purchase for each gift with the properly completed Free Gift Certificate.

084-KFD